The Ruby Heart

Slaves of the New World :2

Ashley Capes

The Ruby Heart

Cover Illiustration: Nick Deligaris
Cover Design: Vivid Covers
Layout & Typeset: Close-Up Books

ISBN-978-0-6483957-0-6

www.ashleycapes.com

Published by Close-Up Books
Melbourne, Australia

For Brooke

Chapter 1

Even from across the square, Thomas was able to mark sweat trickling down the slave's temple, cutting a path through dust and grime. The young man stood on the wooden block before a murmuring crowd. Stock still in his ragged clothing, the man's face was set, jaw clenched, yet there was a smouldering rage to his gaze, as though he were close to exploding into a fit of violence.

And why not?

"We can stop this," Thomas said. He rubbed at a twinge from the newly healed wound in his chest.

Mia rested a hand on his arm, her light touch drawing attention to the fact that it was shaking. "It's too dangerous." Her golden blindfold appeared dull where they stood in the shadows beneath tall buildings. Here in Viterra the walls were mostly iron-clad, dark and cold but even they were warming beneath the late morning sun. They seemed to press in around him, setting his skin to tingling if he drew too near.

"Agreed," Ethan said from Thomas' other side. "And we

need our target here, busy while we liberate his ship. That won't happen if you make a scene now."

Thomas grunted. They were both right of course, but they were wrong too. *And I am just as wrong for agreeing, even though I must.* Each day, Aiden was sailing further and further from Silver Rock. They needed the ship to chase down the *Albion*, and Viterra's port had been closer – and safer – than turning back to Brinhale.

Saving one slave, the first of many who would be sold today, would surely dash their plans. Aside from scaring off their mark, quite a few rather inconvenient guards lined the block, their twin-shots held ready. And more, what would saving one slave achieve? Likely nothing. Yet Thomas stared at the young fellow, noting the straw-coloured hair and then the shape of the man's nose – it had been broken in the past and had healed unevenly. *I will find a way to save you, if no-one else.*

A futile promise? Doubtless so, but the lie he told himself allowed the faint illusion that he was somehow doing what was right, enough so that he fell back into a slouch.

"I don't like it either, Thomas," Mia said.

"I know."

Ethan was still peering at the crowd, searching for Daniels. The so-called noble was supposed to be bidding today but thus far, the human pile of refuse had not appeared. Ethan had described him as a bear of a man but offered little else. *I'll recognise him, don't worry.* Someone of that description ought to have stood out amongst the coats and hats, the slender 'nobles' and the more casual merchants – bearing their coloured sashes unique to Viterra.

At the block, the governor's slave-handler stepped up

beside the slave, who sneered. But the stout fellow only smiled back at his 'property', the greasy expression most unpleasant – especially contrasting as it did with his spotless white shirt and grey vest, the silver buckles on his belt and the polished shoes.

The slave-handler raised a hand for hush and the square quietened. He paused, primping a moment, seeming to relish the attention. "Good people of Viterra, allow me to commence this week's auction with a particularly fine item – his passion speaks of strength, he would be a fine labourer. Or, if any such lord finds themselves a little less conservative in their thinking, a more than suitable Enforcer. Perhaps the Betting House is looking for more strong arms, Lord Tillerson?"

A voice called back from the crowd. "Let's see the whole range, first – I have to watch my spending, you know."

Scattered laughter followed, and the handler winked. "Well then, let's open the bidding and see what old Tillerson can afford, shall we? How about twenty silver pieces? Remember, he is young and strong and has a considerable debt to work off – I estimate it will take ten years at least. This is true value for your coin, lords and ladies."

"What's he done then?" a woman shouted from nearer to Thomas.

"Oh, a misunderstanding is all. It seems he protested a little strongly in one of our finer inns and roughed up the wrong man's son."

Jeers rose from the crowd and hands raised, waving wooden paddles painted with family crests.

"There," Ethan said. "Entering from the left."

A large man, head and shoulders taller than most of the

crowd, his beard like dark tree roots and his black hair just as wild, was parting the people around him without touching a single person – no-one wanted to get in his way. Two thugs followed Lord Daniels, each with rifles slung over their shoulders, and the three stopped before the block.

Daniels didn't seem too interested in the handler's first slave; the angle of the man's head seemed to suggest his eyes were looking beyond. Who was he waiting for? Obviously, the slave-handler wasn't going to open with his most 'prized' slave.

"Time to go," Ethan said.

The rebel leader started from the square, moving into a side-street. Thomas let Mia pass him and watched as she followed. Her vision had still not fully returned; her eyes remained sensitive to light, but she was able to move unaided well enough for the most part. Still, he kept watch as they walked.

Above, the light became patterned where it fell through latticework that extended from the upper storeys. Vines and wisteria spread too, dropping their white and purple petals to the stone, where they were quickly ground into the street.

So far, luck had stayed on their side.

Since fleeing the *Clara*, taking the ruby heart key with them, Ethan had organised transportation at the nearest town and they'd left whatever pursuit Williams was organising far behind. Whoever followed, be it the king himself or his other son Warrick, none could catch Thomas and Mia now. Even if their pursuers guessed they were travelling south – Lord Daniels' ship was about to take them further and faster than any vehicle could manage, even if it was only a coast-hugger.

And the death of Julian would doubtless slow Williams yet further.

Good riddance to bad blood.

Bright light waited at the end of the side street where it opened onto a thoroughfare, the rattle and hiss of steam cars filling the space, only somewhat muffled by the flow of bodies. Ethan joined the stream of people, glancing back to check on them. Now Thomas kept closer to Mia but no-one knocked into her, perhaps noticing his scowl.

A screech rang out at the intersection ahead.

A small, two-man steam car had ground to a halt before a larger vehicle, this one pulling a load of timber on a carriage. The bigger car had a monstrous, puffing boiler and the hawk-shaped herald of the governor – Kensington, another of Williams' puppets.

Drivers were hurling abuse at one another from their seats now, one man half-standing.

"That sounds like something worth detouring," Mia said.

"Indeed. Just two more blocks and we'll reach the waterfront," Ethan replied, then paused before cutting across traffic. Now Thomas took Mia's hand and together they jogged to the other side of the thoroughfare.

The buildings were not so tall now and more bore stone upper-storeys. Factories appeared too – the clang and roar from a steel mill echoed along the street, steam pumping from its stack and the red glow from a mighty blast furnace filling the interior as they passed.

Thomas frowned when his skin tingled once more, and an answering heat seemed to build within him. *Damn Silas, what else is your alchemy doing to me?* His curiosity had not dimmed. And yet, was learning the truth more important than escape? *Not if it means Mia has to stay in this damnable nation.*

Beyond the mill, a group of hulking men in smudged overalls leant against the wall. Smoke rose from pipes and as Thomas drew nearer, he saw that one man's hands were shaking – fingers coated in a pale dust. Powder-rat? If the fellow – or any of them – were in the middle of a star-dust high, then trouble was likely.

And the workers *did* narrow their eyes as they passed but Thomas glared back at them, reaching up to take his twin-shot in hand, pulling it from the sheath strapped to his back. That gave the men pause, though a simmering resentment lingered. Had they seen the yellow hourglass on his wrist?

So it often went with those who bore the white or black.

Ethan, too, had a hand within his vest, no doubt gripping one of the revolvers he carried... but the men did not challenge them, nor did they follow. Their muttering rose, something about the *easy lives of noble slaves* but Thomas ignored them and as they passed, a supervisor roared for the men to return to work.

At the harbour a host of fishing and shipping vessels lined the stone wharves, sails snapping and stacks pumping steam into the blue sky. One ship bore a line of slaves filing down the gangway, overseen by soldiers, while others bore non-human 'cargo' such as rare timber or crates of fish.

Kensington's ship was easily the largest at the dock and while the red-painted *Iron Whale* was no monolith like the *Albion*, being only half the size, it still bore a huge central column and the rail climbed up two storeys. It was doubtless just as Ethan had promised; the only vessel capable of reaching the north. Yet it probably wasn't going to cross any oceans either... and nor would foreign ports accept a Brasatalis vessel even if it could.

Yet they had to try something to find Aiden.

"Did he truly name it the *Iron Whale*?" Mia asked when Thomas finished describing the ship.

"A visionary man," Ethan replied. "Now, all we have to do is wait for the signal."

"I hope your friends are as good as they claim," Thomas said. "And that they remember we're not looking for a bloodbath."

Ethan sighed. "Thomas, you've said this before. You have to trust that I know what I'm doing by now."

"I do," Thomas said. "It's hard to stop worrying."

"So it is," he said, his expression darkening at a commotion further along the busy pier. Twin files of men in dark flak jackets, carrying twin-shot and several also wearing belts with bottle-green canisters attached – smoke grenades. They approached the ship at a jog, spreading out and taking up positions, training their weapons at the *Whale*.

A hush fell across the pier and at the edges of Thomas' vision, he caught a glimpse of people hurrying away.

"What's happening?" Mia asked.

"Something rather bad for Daniels – and us," Ethan muttered.

Chapter 2

About half the men stormed the great ship without ceremony. They coordinated their movements without speaking, with barely even hand-gestures, giving the impression of a well-planned, military assault, as though they'd been watching Daniels' ship for some time perhaps, or had performed such raids before. Shouts from within soon followed and then the boom of rifles.

The soldiers on the waterfront did not react, keeping their weapons trained on the *Iron Whale* and the water.

One man, however, this one bearing the hawk insignia, addressed the onlookers. "Remain calm and keep a safe distance."

"What's happening?" a young voice called.

"Lord Kensington is raiding this ship for star dust – part of his efforts to keep the city safe."

"We should leave," Ethan said. Now his voice was full of repressed frustration as he glared at the city's men.

"Good idea," Thomas replied. "How long will they hold the ship?"

"Forever," he said.

"What do you mean?"

"The *Iron Whale* belongs to Kensington now and its security will be far, far greater than before."

"We need another ship," Mia said.

"I fear so."

"Back to the hotel then?" Thomas asked.

"Right," Ethan replied as he started back into the shadowy side streets. "I'll send word to Leonard and we can plan our next move from the relative comfort of The Bard."

'Relative' was a fair description – it was no dive but nor was it full of luxuries, having only the bare requirements. It was warm enough of a night and the food was good – common Viterra fare, mostly fish and fowl coupled with the dry wine that came from whatever vineyards still flourished this far south.

A gold-painted harp hung above the rusting door to The Bard, the imitation instrument long-since reduced to a dull, scuffed mess. As they started up the small set of steps, a wheezing man exited, his hat and coat slung over one arm. Sweat stained his vest and shirt but he still smiled as he passed. Thomas glanced after the fellow. He hadn't seemed terribly overweight, nor did he have the look of a labourer, what had troubled him so? Surely not the small flight of steps.

The Bard was quiet within, too early for drink or meal, and so only the owner moved about the dining room, sweeping the creaking floorboards in his ill-fitting coat. He nodded to them as they started up the stairs. As elsewhere, the tingle of steel was strong – the rail and support columns, even the roofing beams overhead. As ever, Thomas kept an eye on Mia but she needed no assistance, using the rail as a guide and detouring a hip-sized vase with dead flowers within.

Once inside their room, Mia found her bed and sat, tapping a foot. Ethan began to pace but Thomas took his own cot and lay back, closing his eyes and doing his best to block out the song of the metal around him – even the frame of his cot seemed alive beneath him. Somehow, it helped to smother the disappointment somewhat. They'd come a little too close... and perhaps a ship was the wrong path. Their problem was the same, of course, ship or no, it would be incredibly difficult to track Aiden.

Yet the Bruiser had to return to Silver Rock sooner or later. He couldn't have emptied the entire mine in one trip. *It might be better to steal – or buy – steam-cars and return north that way. Bypass Brinhale... even so, it would take a long time.*

"There's only two other ships worth considering," Ethan said after a moment, the splash of water following. He stood by the basin, towelling off his face and neck. The rebel seemed weary; lines beneath his eyes. "The first, I'm not sure when it will dock and the second is the *Maryana,* Kensington's own ship and the Lord's Wharf is also quite well-protected. Too much for Leonard and his crew, even if you add us."

Thomas sat up. "So where does that leave us?"

"For now, right here at The Bard," Ethan said. "Why don't we get some rest and meet with Leonard in the morning."

"Sounds good to me," Mia said.

Thomas took the first watch, spending the whole time practising ways to block out the call of steel. It was easier if he closed his eyes at first, focused on his own body and not the tingling or heat sensation, sometimes stretching his limbs or digging nails into his palms – as if being forcibly reminded of the flesh and blood was enough to distract whatever part of him was drawn to steel.

Yet when Mia later took his place, it did not seem long before she was waking him.

"Thomas?"

He grumbled. Only her outline appeared, visible before a chink in the curtain that let the streetlight within. There'd been a note of concern in her voice – bringing him all the way to wakefulness.

"What's wrong?"

"We're in danger," she said. "I feel it – Ethan's packing."

Thomas rose, finding his boots and then the twin-shot. "I can check downstairs."

"It's nothing specific," she said. "But someone is coming, and they have ill-intent."

"I'll be back," he said.

She fumbled for his arm. "Thomas—"

"Let me," he said, keeping his voice calm. "We know that I'm the least likely to be hurt, right?" Or, more accurately, the least likely to *instantly* die from a gunshot. If his run-in with Julian was normal now, he'd survive but it would still hurt like hell. *And there's got to be a limit to just how many I can take.*

Still, Mia wasn't going with him, and he was only checking below, nothing more.

"We'll be ready," Ethan said from across the room.

"I'll knock twice," Thomas said.

He placed a hand on the doorknob and clenched his jaw. *No need to rush.* Yet Mia's warning had his pulse racing; she was never wrong. But what danger lurked beyond the door? Kensington? Had Williams' men somehow stumbled upon them? No doubt informants lurked in the city, but none of the posters or listings for escaped slaves in Viterra had seemed to mention Thomas or Mia.

The handle squeaked as it turned, and he exhaled, pausing.

No answering sound from beyond.

He opened the door and still nothing, finally stepping into the hallway. A slither of light slipped from beneath the farthest door but that was all. Only silence from the dining room and kitchen below...

Thomas took a few steps forward, pausing before the shadowy stair. Hadn't there been a pair of creaking boards at the edge of the steps? He crouched, peering toward the darkened windows beside the door.

There, a flash of streetlight on steel.

He strained his ears. A collection of small sounds; the shuffle of feet, something scraping against stone. Someone passing outside? Or hiding? Thomas waited.

"This is the place," a voice said, just audible.

A second voice hissed for quiet and Thomas glanced over his shoulder. Did he have time to warn—

Light bloomed below as a door slammed open. Footsteps thundered after as figures in black poured into The Bard and charged the stairs. At least ten men, and all carrying twin-shot.

"Mia! Ethan! Run!" Thomas roared.

He leapt to the top of the stairs and snatched up the vase, hurling it down. It struck the lead pair, soil flying, and the men collapsed in a jumble of arms, legs and curses. But another half-dozen soldiers charged into the inn amid shouted orders, none of which Thomas heard – he had to stop them, had to buy Mia and Ethan time to escape.

Thomas glanced around. Nothing! His rifle was back in the room and there were no more vases, nothing heavy enough to throw... the roof. Steel support beams lay overhead, one running across the stair. *If I rip it down will we all die?* It wasn't a high ceiling at all... just the room above would be enough.

"Surrender and no-one has to suffer, Thomas," a voice called from the foot of the stairs, an officer. The heaped soldiers were finding their feet. *Out of time.*

Thomas leapt from the landing.

He swung his arms as he did, hands really smacking against the beam and digging in on contact as he tore down with all his strength. A mighty crack followed, and he had just enough time to hear cries of panic, to catch a glimpse of shocked faces, before the ceiling collapsed around him.

Chapter 3

Thomas ground his teeth where he stood. Somehow he'd woken deep within the Sand-Hog, shadows cloaking the faces of those who waited before him, arms folded or weapons raised. The clang of iron and hiss of steam, the pounding tread and booted feet from upper levels and a booming from outside, it all filled his mind – yet the sounds battled with something else, a humming sensation so strong that it interfered with his other senses.

The cold smell of steel seemed to sting his very eyes. Even his skin buzzed as it reacted to the giant, metallic beast around him, bones seeming to twitch within his limbs no matter how he tried to block it out.

Someone was shouting, waving a hand before him.

The fellow wore a black suit... no, flak jacket and mask... and now it appeared to be some sort of tunic crossed by an ammunition belt. The man wore brown leather gloves, and he was speaking, his mouth moving, full of teeth – and then he stood, turning away.

What the hell was happening?

Thomas closed his eyes.

It's the steel; this is too much. It has to stop!

He dug his fingernails into his palms, hard, and the sting of pain skimmed across the surface of his awareness. He ground his jaw and focused on his hands, some of the clamour from the steel receding. Ragged breathing reached his ears; his chest was heaving. He caught a breath and held it a moment, sucking in air through his nose then releasing it slowly.

When he opened his eyes, his vision was still blurry but now a new figure stood before him. Thomas stared, trying to get the details to solidify.

Long, dark curls, a pale face. Green eyes were narrowed, and a frown covered her lips. She turned away. "He's not faking anything." Her voice... a familiar anger; it cut through and he focused on it. *Of course.*

"Elisabeth," he said, blinking repeatedly.

She turned back to him, placing a gloved hand on her hip where a revolver hung on a leather belt. "Yes, Thomas. I see you're finally with us." She unbuttoned her coat with her other hand, revealing the royal W in crimson on the back of the glove. "I suppose you'll be prone to those for some time."

"Why?" he demanded.

Now she smiled – and she should have been beautiful, but the cruelty was stronger. "It takes time for someone as... sensitive as you to adjust to my Sand-Hog, is all. It should be fading, even now."

"You mean, Silas." She was right about the clamour falling away somewhat but he did not want to let her know she was correct. In fact, the less he said the better. *She'll be after Mia soon and I'll be damned if I give her anything.* He could only hope that Mia and Ethan had escaped, that his desperate ploy had been enough. Obviously, having survived suggested that the entire inn hadn't come crashing down.

Elisabeth pulled her revolver. It bore a silver grip and a long line of even scratches on the barrel. She stepped forward and jammed the weapon into his side. Up close, the scent of leather and rose perfume was strong – the steel digging into him was an irritation-only, his skin tingled but she wasn't going to shoot him.

He was too valuable to her master.

"Indeed, Thomas. And now that I seem to have your full attention, let's talk about the future. That hourglass is no memento – you are my property now and I expect obedience. If I do not receive your instant and complete co-operation at all times I can become most unpleasant – as I'm sure you haven't forgotten."

While Elisabeth was only a few years older than he, back when they'd been children in the palace, the difference had been enough that even without her position of power, she had easily been able to inflict all kinds of torment. *The razor cuts and lemon juice were bad enough – what would she come up with now?* Much of it had been fuelled by Julian of course, but it wasn't the threat of the past that gave Thomas pause. He was confident he could overpower her now if need be, but there were simply too many ways she could cause true pain now – chief of which being Mia and Ethan. "You don't have Mia."

Elisabeth winked at him then motioned to one of her men. "Find him a bed and then chain him to it." Then to Thomas, "We'll talk again tomorrow, dear Thomas."

"I'm not your dear," he said to her back.

Elisabeth waved a hand lazily as she passed through the doorway. One of the men gestured with his twin-shot. "Get going."

Thomas preceded the two guards into the hall and started down a dimly-lit corridor lined with steel mesh and occasional ladders leading up. Once, he passed a set of double doors with a carven symbol of fire, a passage to the boilers, no doubt. Just how big was the main boiler? And why an image and not words on the door? A stupid thing to wonder about. *Just focus on your predicament. You can't even try to escape until you know whether Elisabeth has Mia and Ethan. And even if you did know, that's a* lot *of men to take on even for 'The Alchemist's Pet' and by now you're probably a hundred kilometres away from—*

Hands gripped his shoulders and arms. Thomas gave a shout as they flung him up against a wall. He wrenched an elbow free and someone grunted. Blinding pain exploded in the back of Thomas' head then his face was pressed into the steel. He squeezed his eyes shut to try and block the tingling, now more like being peppered with gravel. "I have a few things to add to Lady Elisabeth's remarks," a soft voice spoke – as though the man stood a few feet back, and wasn't the one holding Thomas, who had no way to turn his head and see the speaker.

"I hope you're going to admit that you know Williams wants me alive."

"Oh, that he does," the man said, tone dripping with treacle. "And I support him of course. But believe me, a lot of healing can occur between now and when that time comes."

Thomas said nothing, as the threat did not seem idle.

"While Lady Elisabeth commands this tank, you will also

receive orders from the king himself – orders which I will deliver and which you are expected to carry out in secret."

"Why?" *Who is this fool? What does Williams want that he simply cannot ask Elisabeth to provide?* Something troubling was afoot on the Sand-Hog.

"Let me worry about why."

"And do you expect me to split myself in two when my orders contradict one another?"

A soft chuckle, like the rustling of dry leaves. "I can't ever imagine such a thing happening."

Thomas frowned as best he could with his face being mostly squashed. "And those orders?"

"To do as Elisabeth instructs... for now."

"Or?"

A sigh followed. "Aside from the extensive bodily harm we have already discussed there are a number of those you care about whom might be... reduced."

"I only care for Mia and you do not have her," Thomas said. "And even if you did, you cannot hurt her. Williams wants more than her powers."

"Yes, yes. Her womb is also of most interest to His Majesty but I am sure she could bear a child without fingers, yes? And don't overlook the others." The man paused. "Ethan and the other rebels, Henry from Silver Rock, and even the marsh people. Thomas, there are so many we might use as leverage."

How does this slimy bastard know so much? Thomas hesitated before answering. "Only if you actually have them."

Yet it seemed his doubt was noted by William's spy, by the grin that entered his voice. "We will speak again, Thomas." Footsteps started to recede. "Lock him in."

"Yes, sir," replied one of his captors.

One man moved to a nearby door, rattling with a key a moment. The squeak and grind of heavy hinges followed and then Thomas was shoved inside toward a dark corner. His shin crashed into something hard and he swore. *Something to go with other aches and bruises from my little stunt in The Bard.*

"Keep it quiet," a gruff voice said as light followed – one of them held a lamp. "Now sit."

A steel-framed bed rested before him and he sat as another man dragged a heavy set of manacles into the room, bending to affix them to one of Thomas' legs. The cold steel was heavy and instead of tingling, it gave off a sense of... closeness. As though, it was almost *bonding* with Thomas' leg.

Then he left, leaving only one fellow behind.

"You probably think you can break these, right?" Gruff-Voice grinned, revealing a single missing tooth. "Well, you can't because The Alchemist made them special. So don't bother trying. And do exactly what the Lady says. Same goes for The Fox."

"The Fox?"

"Right. And if you think Lady Elisabeth is something to worry about, trust me, slave, Fox is far worse."

Chapter 4

Two bridges stood before Mia, a pair of silver streaks hovering over a churning river of navy blue. The tips of the water were black instead of white, the sky above cloaked in clouds whose edges had turned iridescent, as if a vast sun waited beyond each one.

She stepped toward the left bridge and a tiny Sand-Hog rattled forth – no taller than her knee. A woman drove the Hog from a platform; dark curls enshrouded her entire form. When she steered the Hog away from Mia, a body that had been tied to the machine bounced after, covered in a shimmering red – Mia gasped.

"Thomas!"

She knew without recognising features – she *knew*.

Yet the figure did not respond to her cry and when Mia gave chase one of his limbs broke free with an ear-piercing crack, and then another and third until she fell to her knees, turning to scramble back for the second bridge, panting as her hands tore at the dirt.

She stopped, gulping back a sob.

Here, Thomas waited at the other end, seated across from the same woman – from Elisabeth.

His expression was one of determination, concealing fear perhaps. He was as he always appeared to Mia: strong and kind, his brown hair cut short and his face hovering between the boy she remembered clearly and the man she imagined him to now be.

The two were arguing. Mia could not make out the words but whenever Thomas spoke, Elisabeth's hair twisted and frayed, parts thinning to drift away but at her every answer Thomas was the one who changed. He shrunk back, face turning grey as stone and his limbs becoming mightily still.

Behind them both, the *Clara* loomed in a half-realised shape, as if appearing from a cloud of swirling fog.

Mia rose to charge forward, but her steps were as nothing; she never drew closer and Thomas and Elisabeth remained locked in their apparent stalemate. Yet when Mia glanced over to the first silvery bridge, the Sand-Hog remained in place; Thomas tied behind, not unlike a torn hunk of meat now that he'd lost his limbs. She shuddered, backing away as her stomach churned, bile rising up her throat.

And then her feet found nothing, and she was falling.

***

"Mia, are you all right?"

She flinched, reaching for the bridge... and found flesh instead. Someone squeezed her hands, speaking softly.

"You're safe."

Mia exhaled long and slow as the vision faded and the

darkness returned. Before her, Ethan was little more than a dark outline beyond her blindfold. Light came in from behind, streaming through an open window of the small town's inn, and though it was little, a flicker of hope came with it. But she pushed it down. *Maybe if I don't hope too much I truly will regain my sight.*

Maybe.

"Was it a nightmare?" Ethan asked.

"A vision." She exhaled. Ethan's scent; a mix of leather and faint sweat grew stronger as he sat beside her. "I think we need to turn back."

"I know we can't keep up, but I don't think you really mean that. We know the Hog's direction. It leaves a clear trail—"

"No, I mean I think it's too dangerous for Thomas. I saw... if we follow, I believe he will die. If we don't, I see him in a stalemate with Elisabeth but at least he lives. I even saw the *Clara* behind them."

Ethan was silent a moment. "Ah."

"Do you doubt it?" She didn't; not once had her feelings or visions, as they sometimes were, steered her or Thomas wrong. Not once since the day they'd begun, not long after their first escape.

"Hardly. I just wish there was a way."

"Perhaps I simply haven't seen it yet."

"Then what now?"

"I think we need to return to our search." Mia reached for the ruby heart where it hung on a chain around her neck, the hard edges warm beneath her grip. If she could somehow find a pilot as they'd first planned, could she save Thomas that way? Turning away from his trail seemed madness but wasn't that why her vision had shown the airship? It was obvious. *But even if you've never been wrong you don't always know what the visions mean at first, do you?*

If she *did* follow her vision and somehow made a mistake, she'd be taking herself farther and farther from Thomas...

"Are you sure?"

There was still a trace of worry in his voice and if she'd been able to see his face it would have been a mirror, surely, but she still nodded.

"Then we could probably turn north and cross the waste. Try for a ship in Brinhale."

"We'd have to keep out of Williams' clutches."

"There are also rumours of a ship, locked in an ancient dock. I don't know how reliable they are... but supposedly it's only a few days south of here."

"The *Angelique*? Isn't it a myth?" Although, even if it was something of a fairy tale she first heard from maids in the palace as a child, so too had the *Clara* once been.

"It might be," he said, and it seemed he shrugged by the shift in his outline. "Much closer than Brinhale if we wanted to at least check it out."

"Thomas and I have never travelled so far south... I only know of the *Angelique* as a child's tale. Williams' family would have taken it if it was useful and locked it away like the *Clara* if they couldn't use it, right?"

"It's very possible."

She sighed. "Somehow it seems easier than chasing down Aiden."

"We could at least start in the fishing port of Tamas. Perhaps someone there will have more information. Or maybe they've even caught a glimpse of the *Albion*? If not, we still have the steam-car."

"True." Despite the confidence she professed in her visions, she now found the words that would set her aside from the Sand-Hog's trail difficult to speak. Finally, she stood. *Trust it as you always have.* Thomas would understand. Visions aside, Williams wanted him alive for the Colossus. Even if it felt wrong, she knew what would happen if she followed – the image of Thomas' tiny blood-stained corpse bouncing behind the Sand-Hog flashed.

"Mia?"

"Let's find the *Angelique* then."

Chapter 5

Days wore into one another with the grind and rumble of movement for company, the hum of the steel, which he was steadily mastering, broken only by simple meals of bread, dried fruit and water, and a predictably dull array of cursing from soldiers – 'freak' featured most prominently in their efforts.

Thomas soon learnt the limits of his freedom. As the guard had promised, his chains were unbreakable – Silas had truly forged them, it seemed. The fact was, it remained impossible to feel his way into any sort of affinity with them; they seemed glued to his leg despite not actually moulding themselves close.

The chains did allow him to cross from one side of his room – his cell – and back, which meant his chamber pot was far enough away that he was allowed some token of respite. Otherwise, it was a bed with a single heavy blanket and pillow, little else of note. An empty wooden desk where he ate but nothing of use. No weapons, no tools, nothing.

And always doubt gnawed at him.

Did they truly have Mia? Or had she and Ethan escaped? Keeping Mia and the ruby heart away from Williams was more important than his own freedom but he couldn't know if Elisabeth was even now speeding toward Brinhale.

She might be doing so even without Mia on board. The king would no doubt still want a pilot for the Colossus – even, most likely – if Thomas had killed Julian. Fox and Elisabeth both seemed to have similar orders and no hints at meting out any sort of punishment or revenge on behalf of the king for Julian's death. Of course, the old snake might well be saving that for a face-to-face meeting.

And more, had Thomas ruined the king's plans for Mia? Or would Williams pass on that role to Warrick? Or simply seek to impregnate Mia himself? Thomas growled at the thought. *The only way that will come to pass is over my dead body.*

Footsteps beyond his cell approached and he straightened; his usual mealtime was not for some hours.

A bolt slid free and then the door ground open. Light followed – this time, natural light from open portholes. Thomas raised an arm. *Still stings the eyes.*

"The Lady wants to see you."

It was Gruff-voice.

"I don't want to see her."

"Too bad," the guard said as he entered, key in hand. Two men followed, each holding twin-shots. Serious stuff in the close-confines of the Sand-Hog. Gruff-voice inserted the key and the lock clicked open. "No sudden movements, now," he warned.

Thomas followed them out into the bright hall, squinting as he did, unable to catch much of a glimpse of the outside before he was prodded up a ladder. The cold steel steps tingled beneath his grip but only just enough to notice.

The upper levels bore more cladding on the walls, similar-sized windows but he now walked across burnished steel and passed well-appointed rooms; what appeared to be a sitting room with silent instruments, a library and, in what he guessed was the centre of the Hog, a sprawling dining hall with long benches and a darkened kitchen, enough seating for over a hundred men.

Beyond waited another climb – this one shorter, a flight of steps lined with a deep but worn red runner, led up to another hall now with closed doors and finally a hatch. From his estimation, it would be a fourth level or the deck.

"She's waiting," Gruff-voice said.

Thomas turned the handle easily and a mutter from behind him followed; maybe it was harder for them. He kept a dour grin to himself and pushed the hatch open, a welcome gust of air swirling in, bringing the low rumble of the engines with it. When he climbed free, he found himself on a wide deck, the steel railings broken by two shapes – a Gatling gun and a woman, dark hair flowing in the breeze.

What a picture – and there's not a decent bone in her entire body.

He pulled himself the rest of the way free, breathing deeply. *Fresh air at least – even if it tastes a little like dust, it's better than the cell.* He glanced behind, but the soldiers weren't following. Did Elisabeth want privacy? Or was it more of her posturing? A reminder that she needed no guard?

Beyond her figure stretched a pale horizon of swirling dust. It was after noon and the sun seemed... wrong for a trip north. They were heading west? A thin tendril of smoke caught his eye – it came from a scattered ruin; the wastes were like a giant land one step removed from a graveyard. What few people survived here tended to huddle in the crumbling stones, scavenging useable steel and other items to sell in Viterra or at the garrison towns on the border.

"Join me," Elisabeth called.

He strode to the rail and gripped it in both hands, looking across at her. "Where is Mia?" He pitched his voice over the engine and the crunch of the tread where it cut through sandy wastes, but her reply was easy enough to hear.

"My men tell me you constantly badger them with questions about her."

"Let me see her."

"So you can plan an escape together? I don't think so, Thomas – have you somehow grown stupider since you escaped?" She still hadn't bothered to look at him.

Thomas lashed out, catching her by the throat. His free hand snapped over her wrist when she reached for her revolver. "What do you think, *Lady*?"

But the shock on her face faded quickly, replaced by a strained grin. "Do you really think we're alone?" She looked over his shoulder.

He glanced back and saw a man on the small canon-deck above; he held a magnifier-rifle, the barrel trained on Thomas' back.

"See?"

Thomas clenched his jaw, even as he released her.

Elisabeth rubbed at her throat then shook her head. "Fool."

He turned back to the empty plain. "I suppose you'd have

to have family to understand."

She joined him with a weary sigh. "Use that thick head for a change, will you? I've brought you up here for a reason."

"Being?"

"I've planned a little detour before we return to Brinhale and I suspect you'll prove quite useful. If you cooperate without committing the very acts I must warn you about over and over, I will let you see Mia – for a single meal, with me. Under guard of course."

Thomas frowned – not at the offer, but at the mention of a detour. Fox was still somewhere aboard, what would he think of such news? Would he expect something? *My situation isn't improving yet.*

"Well?" she asked.

"What proof do I have?"

"None, of course. And you can take it or leave it, but refusal will simply mean another few weeks in the cell." Elisabeth shrugged. "When you've made up your mind, tell one of your guards."

"That's not—"

"Do as I say," she barked, and Thomas frowned at the sudden flash of anger in her eyes.

"As you wish." He started back for the hatch, glancing up at the rifleman. The fellow was tracking Thomas' every step with his weapon.

Chapter 6

A heroic burst of steam surged from the tank as the Sand-Hog rumbled to a complete halt before the dust-caked walls of Last Castle. The town had a thrown-together look where it spread along the banks of the Buyo River, which was in turn fed by the mighty, snow-capped peaks of the distant Crenthrowe Mountains. It was the final chance to take on water before venturing into the desert.

Runaway slaves flocked to Last Castle despite its large garrison, hoping to buy passage to the Inland Federation. Sometimes it was possible. Thomas remembered one runaway, a thin woman with some skill at healing who'd found work on a black-market caravan heading west.

Of course, no-one had wanted to take on Thomas and the 'burden' of his sister.

Nearest the walls, a large iron gate stood open, admitting scavengers with the morning sun. No travelling merchants today, it seemed, but no doubt Elisabeth and her soldiers would soon make up for the relative quiet. If not them, perhaps a patrol.

She stood before a pair of older men, one with silvery hair and the other a shaven head, explaining her orders and gesturing to the town. Other soldiers hurried along the decking or in the corridors below, doubtless preparing to disembark or perhaps drawing straws for who would stay behind to guard the Sand-Hog. Not that anyone would be foolish enough to storm it, but Elisabeth didn't strike him as one to take needless risks.

Does she truly have Mia on board?

Thomas waited, two men flanking him; neither guard was Gruff, but both equally close-mouthed. If only he was able to break Silas' damn chains. Finally, Elisabeth looked his way, then sent the silver-haired soldier to him.

"Lady says you're to help. Says you know what will happen if you try anything stupid. That right?" His brow was drawn into a frown and his sweeping moustache seemed to twitch in the breeze.

"I do. What am I needed for?" he asked, though he could guess.

"Heavy lifting."

Thomas folded his arms. "Water?"

"Right. Stick at my side and there won't be any problems. Once we've loaded the Hog, you're back in your cell. Understood?"

"Yes."

"Good. Let's hurry it up then," he said, and started toward the nearest ladder.

Elisabeth lifted her voice. "Do listen to Sergeant Wilkins, won't you, Thomas?"

He didn't answer, only started climbing after the soldier.

Once Thomas hit the ground, a tiny puff of dust following,

he sighed. Just having his feet on earth, just having a little distance from Elisabeth was enough to ease a knot of tension between his shoulders – one he hadn't realised had been building ever-since her claim about Mia.

Am I a fool to even consider she's telling the truth?

Obviously, any lie about Mia was going to be an effective way to control him. He glanced back up at the Hog, sand still trickling from its tread. What if Mia truly was inside somewhere? He couldn't afford to do anything rash. *No need to give up either.* A chance for escape would come, he just had to keep his eyes open.

Once the dozen men had gathered, Sergeant Wilkins led them toward the town walls at a brisk walk. The sun bore down on Thomas, warm but not yet unbearable. The murmur and hum from the town soon swelled as they passed through the decaying but still formidable gates and entered paved streets. Scavengers in their threadbare clothing moved from stall to stall in the gate-market, and richer merchants or residents conducted their own business too, most of them with overburdened slaves in tow. Unlike the scavengers, these people wore a better cut of cloth and often carried revolvers, compared to the few willow rifles seen on the waste-landers.

Federation folk were more common here too – when a striking woman with darker skin and dreadlocks dressed in a snug dress passed them by, Wilkins' men gave low whistles. She ignored them, along with one man's comment about "finding her sister" at one of the brothels.

"Do your damn job first," Wilkins snapped.

The men fell silent and Thomas grinned at the fellow who'd spoken loudest.

"What are you smiling about, slave?" The fellow glared at him. A shiny scar ran from cheek to jaw.

"You, obviously."

The soldier blinked, then spat. "You'd better shut your trap before I do it for you."

Thomas stared back, simply letting his grin widen.

One of scar-face's friends held him back and after a short scuffle, the Sergeant stepped before the man. "Get a grip, Benjamin." Then he turned to Thomas. "You, walk beside me."

Thomas complied but spoke no further. Maybe he was pushing his luck, even if it felt pretty damn good. Taking his frustration out on those who guarded him probably wasn't the smartest move, but he had to do something with it rather than let it fester.

The sergeant led them beyond the square and into cooler streets shadowed by the upper stone storeys of the buildings, some tidy-looking hotels and other merchants, a dress maker and cobbler. The rowdier buildings – the taverns and brothels – were closer to the river on the opposite side of town but even as they travelled that direction, Sergeant Wilkins took them to a squat building of dark stone that bore a military-look with its heavy steel door and grated windows.

A broad set of steps led down to a giant basement, to a room lit by narrow ground-floor windows and more than a few lamps. A wide desk sat in the centre of the room; flanked by twin barrels on either side. They bore the royal W, and the swift strokes, he assumed, were markings meant to represent one of the river towns further south.

Two women sat together at the desk, one writing in a

ledger and the other watching their approach. Both wore spectacles and had similar dark hair tied in a bun – and as he neared, Thomas saw they that were not just similar, but twins.

He blinked. Twins? He hadn't seen twins in years and years; so few seemed to be born anymore.

Wilkins hailed them. "Ladies, I hope you can accommodate us, I know it is an unannounced visit."

"Of course, Sergeant," one said with a smile. "We haven't seen you for quite some time."

The other woman continued to write. "How much would you like?"

"Well, my lady has been quite busy up north," he said. "We're going to need enough for a return trip from the Federation."

The first woman raised a feathery eyebrow. "Hunting runaways again?"

"King's business, I'm afraid."

"As it always is, Sergeant. One day I'd love it if you surprised us with a frank answer for a change. Just to keep things interesting."

Thomas clenched his jaw at their casual back and forth. How easy it seemed for them to pretend they weren't a part of William's dark world of slavery. And how disconcerting to see them smile as they conducted business, as though it were all perfectly natural. Normal. *They're all as bad as each other, even if they don't personally own any slaves.*

And yet, it was nothing he wasn't already well aware of.

Only the reminders were becoming far less tolerable.

Wilkins had finished his business and was waving everyone left of the counter where a broad set of double doors waited. A winding sound followed, and the doors creaked open, revealing an empty platform.

The sergeant pointed, explaining for Thomas' benefit, no doubt. "Water is stored below – it's our job to transport it from here to the Hog. You'll take a trolley to yourself and you'll do several trips. I don't expect any complaints and for your sake, don't spill a single drop of the king's water."

"I see."

They filed into the elevator and rode in silence until it came to a halt. Wilkins hauled the doors open once more, revealing a sprawling room now only dimly-lit. A chill lay upon the air; it seemed to come from large copper pipes and broad spouts, some of which poured water into 44-gallon drums that rested on a track of some manner.

Men in overalls, their tattoos difficult but not impossible to discern in the poor light, moved between pipes, monitoring the water flow it seemed. They soon reached up to a round handle to close the valve. Then, one signalled to someone across the room, who set to work turning a lever, at which point the barrels moved, the track lurching into motion. When the barrels reached the opposite end of the room, they were loaded onto a sturdy steel trolley and then a pair of men pushed them, wheels rattling, across the floor toward the lift.

Armed guards, no doubt supplied by the Last Castle garrison, oversaw the entire process, few with weapons drawn – most happy to chuckle along with whatever rot Wilkins' men were telling them.

"You've got good timing, Sergeant," an older man on the trolley said as he passed. "We'll be ready for your first lot soon."

"Thanks, Anders."

And even though Anders did not return at once, the man was right, since the next pair of men handed off their load to Wilkins' crew, and the next and the next, sending three up in the lift.

Then came a trolley for Wilkins and the remaining soldier and finally Thomas' own trolley. One of the slaves paused. "This is heavy, even for a big guy."

"He'll be fine," Wilkins called.

The fellow shrugged, turning back to his work.

Thomas gripped the handle and braced himself before leaning into the task. The trolley seemed lighter than it should have, despite a load that probably twice exceeded his own mass – he was actually able to move it, not without effort, but nor was it impossible.

Silas' ghostly hand once more? No doubt had the trolley and drums been of wood he'd not have had as much luck. Thomas started after Wilkins and the lift ascended, this time stopping at street level, and they exited into a broad side street then joined a thoroughfare heading toward the gates.

"All right, men. The sooner we're done, the sooner you get to waste that hard-earned coin in town," Wilkins said, his words met by a small cheer.

Thomas followed the others across the paved streets, keeping to one side so as to let the occasional steam car and other traffic pass. The wheels of his trolley were solid, handling the terrain well enough, though the stretch of earth between the walls and the Hog were tough, eliciting a wide-ranging array of curses from the soldiers.

But they returned the empty trolleys to Williams' water

merchant and repeated the process once more, then again until the morning wore into noon and then beyond, by which point Thomas' arms and legs were beginning to flag, even with his strength. The only change in the monotony of the task was when a patrol from the garrison did ride out, and it was easily two hundred soldiers. Thomas had shaken his head. *Just how many men are stationed here if that's a patrol? Far more than last time, surely.*

Now, no-one bothered to curse; they saved their breath for their work until finally Wilkins took the empty trolley from him where they stood beneath the Hog's loading ramp.

"Inside then," he said. "Someone will be waiting to take you to your cell – and I'll be watching you climb."

Thomas started to the ladder, pausing a moment to rest his limbs, then he climbed.

"Enjoy the stink of your own shit," a voice sailed up after him.

Thomas turned.

It was the man who'd been reprimanded by Wilkins earlier and now his friends were laughing and slapping him on the back. Thomas offered an obscene gesture then resumed his climb; he didn't have the energy to return and give the man a thrashing. Assuming he'd even have the chance.

Still, the soldier had marked himself for some special attention whenever Thomas escaped. *If* he escaped.

Yet, at least now he'd have a chance to finally discover the truth – did Elisabeth truly have Mia? The doubt returned. Wouldn't he have been able to feel her presence somehow? They'd barely spent half a day apart since they'd first escaped; it seemed like he always knew – at least roughly – where she was, even if that had only meant a half-realised possible sense of direction...

A black-haired soldier met him at the top.

"Come on, then," the man said, irritation clear in his voice.

"I need a moment," Thomas said as he caught his breath.

"Do you? See if I give a shit about what you need," he said, reaching out to grip Thomas' shoulder.

Thomas glared at the man. "Let go."

"All right, slave. Here's your first lesson. Do as I say and do it *when* I say or—"

Thomas pivoted and aimed a kick at the back of the man's knee.

The fellow collapsed with a shout and Thomas fell after the soldier, landing with a forearm across the man's throat. Thomas applied pressure as the big-mouthed fool struggled. "Listen, meat-bag. I said I needed a moment. Now, I might be a slave but I'm worth something to the old man up in Brinhale – are you?"

A shot cracked the air, bullet ricocheting off the nearby deck.

Thomas looked up to see a fellow with a magnifier peering down at them, the barrel aimed at his chest. *Same guy from before or a replacement?* The soldier called down. "That's your only warning. The next one punches through your shoulder. You'll live but it won't be pretty."

"Fine."

Thomas stood, hauling the soldier up by the front of his jacket, and then, while the man was still mostly off balance – gave a shove.

The soldier clattered to the decking once more. Thomas strode toward the hatch then knelt to wrench it open, glancing back to his jailor, who was scrambling to his feet, face flushed with anger. Thomas raised an eyebrow. "Need a moment?"

Chapter 7

The scent of dust lay heavy on the air as it rushed across her cheeks. The goggles and her blindfold, which now covered her mouth, did their job as the car thumped along the old road. Not so sunken as the path she and Thomas had used in the marsh, not by any stretch, but it was still no royal highway either. *This is hard work on my tailbone.*

Little was discernible save for a general brightness of the afternoon sky compared to the horizon but according to Ethan, they were nearing Tamas.

"I see the haze of smoke and the ocean beyond it."

"I've been thinking, Ethan. Are we likely to be welcomed?" she asked. "Thomas and I had always avoided Tamas – supposedly they're all pirates and thieves and not a single big steamship in the port. Have you been there?"

"Well, one man's pirate is another's freedom-fighter... but it can be a rough place, I have to admit."

"Sounds ideal for recruiting."

"Well, I do know someone there, so we'll see what she can do."

Mia smiled. "Seems you know someone everywhere."

"I'm blessed by many friends," he said, pausing a moment. It seemed he'd been about to speak again but when she turned her head, the vague shadow of his outline seemed to be focused on the road.

Was he holding something back? "Ethan?"

A sigh was nearly lost beneath the engine. "I wanted to say that you and Thomas were on that list... I wasn't sure if I should remind you. If that was cruel of me."

"It's fine, truly. I trust the vision," Mia said. "And thank you," she added quickly.

He nodded, and she couldn't help but want him to answer instead. That way, she'd be able to read his voice, to know whether he truly believed in their decisions, but when he did speak again, sometime later, he sounded at ease.

"We're nearing the town. Once inside I'll find Delilah and we can start searching for any truth behind the rumours."

"Will she know much about the *Angelique*?"

"I think so. She's been around long enough," he said. "She's the Mistress of the Sea."

"Which is?"

"An oddly poetic way of saying she's the town undertaker – she handles burial at sea."

"They truly call her that?"

"It's a Tamas thing, I suspect."

Ethan soon slowed the car, the boiler's muted hiss easing as the wheels bumped up onto stone and tall shadows rose around them. *Buildings.* Even over the sound of the car jaunty music played on fiddles and horns – an odd mix – reached her, followed by a few shouts, rough voices, but shouts of happiness rather than disagreement.

And beneath it all the scent of salt on the air, the distant, almost-imperceptible roar of the ocean. *Like returning to Silver Rock.* She breathed in and the sizzle of spiced meat followed, replaced just as quickly by dust as Ethan bought the steam-car to a halt.

"This is Delilah's place – we're in a yard behind her building. Hers is the two-storey; I wish I could show you the view from her balcony," he said as he exited.

Mia pulled the handle and stepped down, keeping a hold of the door a moment. Delilah's building was little more than a wide shadow, lighter greys around it. "It's almost enough just to smell the sea once more." She reached back into the car and lifted the willow rifle free, both as an aid and to have a weapon. *Friend or no, it always pays to be prepared.* After all, Aiden's appearance at Silver Rock was an obvious lesson; no doubt Ethan carried his revolvers at least.

Mia followed him across level ground, her rifle questing before her. As Ethan's footsteps paused, she slowed and then his boots were climbing steel steps. Her barrel clicked against a hand-rail and then she was climbing too.

At the top, Ethan called out with the rapping of knuckles against wood. "Javier, are you in? It's Ethan." He knocked again, then waited.

"What if no-one's home?" Mia asked.

"I doubt they'd be far – Javier usually does most of the day-to-day errands within a few blocks at most."

Footsteps soon sounded from beyond the door and a soft squeak of the handle turning followed. "Ethan?"

"None other."

"Well, it's been years – I'm surprised to see you alive," said a deep voice.

"Not as surprised as me," he replied. "I've come to see her.

My friend and I hope to impose upon her vast memory. Is she in?"

"She's cooking – let me take you both," Javier said, and it seemed by the sound of his words that he smiled.

There was less light inside and now Mia found her rifle clicking against some sort of polished stone – marble perhaps. *Impressive. Just how much money's in the funeral business?*

"Can I help you, lady?" Javier asked.

"I'll be fine, so long as neither of you run ahead," she replied.

He laughed. "No fear of that."

"How is she?" Ethan asked as they walked. His question echoed as if down a long corridor.

"Well, Ethan. I suspect she will outlive us all – as if the spirits of those she sends to sea somehow sustain her beyond natural years."

"That's very mystical of you."

He chuckled again. "To my surprise, I think I am changing." His steps slowed. "And here we are." A door creaked, and Javier called out. "Del, you have some visitors – Ethan and a companion."

"Send them in!"

Delilah's voice seemed both pleased and somewhat preoccupied, and by the slight rasp, Mia guessed the woman was elderly. As before, Mia's feet brushed on polished stone but now there was a dull glow, as if from a bank of windows. Water bubbled and the rich smell of curried meat, perhaps chicken, filled the room.

"Ethan? My, my, you're still with us? The Gods must fancy you." For its age, her voice was quite musical, and it seemed she was seated – perhaps on a stool before her stove.

"If they're out there I hope they do, Delilah," Ethan said. "I'm glad you're still here too."

"Course I am. How about your friend? Going to introduce her to me or not?"

"And you're as patient as ever too," he said. "This is Mia."

A slight steel creaking followed and a soft hand gripped Mia's own. Delilah's voice came from a point that suggested she was still seated or either very short... or perhaps she was in a wheeled-chair? "Pleased to meet you, dear. I hope Ethan hasn't dragged you into one of his capers."

"No, not truly. I fear I've caused the trouble."

"I only half believe it, girl. He's enough trouble for everyone. Now come, let's all sit and you can tell me what's happening."

Despite the absence of any warning feelings, Mia kept her story brief, focusing on their escape but holding back the true nature of her or Thomas' gifts, and mentioning only the need to escape.

"So we've come here in the hope that you can help us find something, if it truly exists," Ethan added.

"And what would that be?" she said over the clink of a spoon being placed down.

"The *Angelique*."

"Ah. To be honest, I'm not sure it does – people around here have long *wanted* it to be true and I hear search parties still set out from time to time but all return empty-handed."

"No further clues have returned?"

"Well, that's up for debate. You could ask Christopher, if he's still around. I can send Javier to rustle him up if you wish."

"Please."

"Very well. While we wait, you can join me for a meal. I take you need lodgings as well."

"If you'd be as kind as I've come to expect, that would be wonderful," Ethan said.

"Bah. I'll expect you to do your share. Both of you," she added.

"Of course, and thank you," Mia replied.

"Careful," Ethan said. "She's likely been saving something truly unpleasant for unwary travellers like us."

Delilah chuckled. "Let's eat first, then we can talk about what you'll owe me."

Chapter 8

"Now, you'll be sleeping down the hall from Javier, so if you need something wake him as I need my beauty sleep. I'm assuming one room is enough?" Delilah said; a slight echo to her voice from the corridor they stood within, Mia on aching feet. Ethan had been put to work in the yard and Mia had worked the kitchen over.

"Ah..." Mia felt a flush at the woman's words, turning to where Ethan stood beside her.

He cleared his throat. "Actually, two rooms might be best."

Delilah cackled with laughter. "If you say so, kids. Come then, Mia. Just a little further for you."

Mia followed the sound of the old woman's wheels and it seemed that Ethan watched her, but she didn't speak... and she didn't know why. *Nothing's changed, has it? I'm thinking and acting like a teenager all of a sudden. Why? Because of a simple misunderstanding?*

"Here we are," Delilah said, taking Mia's hand and guiding it to the doorknob.

"I'm fine, but thank you," she replied gently. Behind her,

Ethan's door clicked closed.

"I wonder about that," Delilah said, lowering her voice.

"What do you mean?"

"Surely you feel his gaze upon you, girl? I know you're not stupid, so what is it? Worried about your brother finding out? Worried you won't know what to do?"

Mia frowned. "What to do?"

"With a man."

Again, she flushed and the sensation that Delilah found her discomfort amusing only made it worse. *Get a grip, Mia.* She steeled her jaw. "Your hospitality has suddenly grown colder."

"Hush, girl. I'm not mocking you – I just want you to realise what you haven't seen for yourself. It's plain on your face, even with that blindfold. I see it when you listen to him and I see it when he looks at you. And Ethan's a good man, despite his half-dozen flaws."

Is she right? "Well, thank you for the room." Mia opened the door and slipped inside, closing it as quickly as seemed polite, then leant against the wood a moment. A weary sigh followed. Whatever was happening could wait until the morning.

She let her pack slide to the floorboards then placed her willow rifle across it before moving into the room, slowly, in the darkness. There was only the faintest hint of light where curtains must have stood. Off to the right, as she neared, the sense of something low. The bed no doubt. She bent and found the hard edges, then soft blankets.

Perfect.

Mia sat, kicked off her shoes and climbed in before removing her blindfold. Then she stretched out and closed her eyes. Sleep would wipe the confusion away, surely.

Yet her mind did not want to cooperate.

Even back when she'd first met him in the rebel camp, Ethan *had* seemed to pay her extra attention. She'd noticed, of course she had, especially looking back now. *But there's so much else to deal with, and that hasn't changed. I need to find Aiden and then rescue Thomas. I don't have room for... whatever Delilah thinks is going to happen.* She rolled onto her side. *And if your past is anything to go on...*

Despite her worry, sleep did eventually drift down – her limbs were heavy after helping Delilah and the tension of waiting for Christopher to arrive had obviously taken its toll too.

But though sleep came it brought no rest.

Mia found herself in a cold room of dark, gleaming stones, each drop of moisture tinted blue where it clung to the walls. Somewhere, a clock ticked – an echoing, decayed sound. Before her, figures lay stretched upon low tables, twitching beneath blankets of woven seaweed – yet there was no stench.

"Talk to us," a voice reverberated.

She stepped forward and lifted the nearest blanket.

Beneath, a young woman in a smock, her bare feet restless. She had no face, instead it was a blank wall of skin with a subtle peak where a nose might have rested and a painted rune, like a curving X that stretched from cheek to cheek.

"I am Mia."

"We know," the same voice replied, and Mia wasn't sure which, if any, of the bodies had spoken. Three other shapes were in the room, each covered in seaweed, each twitching slightly.

"Do you want me to help you?"

"No need – just hear our warning."

"I will."

"You cannot find a pilot; you must make one."

She straightened. "*Make* one? Is this a riddle?"

"Riddle? It is plain as the day – heed the words; they are clearer than any vision afforded by your Farsight, are they not?"

"Farsight? Is that the true name of my gift – did it come from my parents?"

The room began to shimmer, and the twitching of the bodies ceased.

"Wait, please – can you tell me anything else?"

A soft darkness was bleeding through the stones, rising from the floor and bringing a sudden chill with it, strong enough that she shivered. "Wait!" Mia stumbled for the next table, only for her limbs to snag in the very air.

"Enjoy the warm days, Mia."

***

She woke to a knocking on her door.

"Mia, may I come in?"

Ethan.

She sat up, blinking away the last shreds of the dream. Was it morning already? She tied her blindfold and sat up. "Of course."

The vague grey of new light entered the room, Ethan's familiar profile revealed in the doorway, hesitating a moment. *Because of what Delilah said? Or is it something else and I'm just thinking too much?* "Christopher is here; he's waiting for us with Delilah. Maybe we'll get some answers." His tone seemed as it always did; relaxed, not too far from delivering a quip of some sort.

"Good," she said. She nearly mentioned the misunderstanding, yet the search for the *Angelique* came first. Even the dream, troubling as it was, could wait at least a little longer for the *Clara* was far, far away indeed. "Is there a basin here?"

"Right across from you," he said.

Even as she found her way to it, splashing water across her face, there was a lingering doubt. Why had the dead spoken to her? Were they meant to be bodies below, perhaps those that hadn't been sent to sea yet? Her Gift – apparently Farsight – was hardly limited to visions, it seemed. *I'll ask Ethan to take me to the basement later.* "So, what's he like?"

"A bit of a corsair if you ask me; but he knows the southern waters well, all the towns too. I wish you could see his coat, its golden trim is quite magnificent."

"Can we trust him?"

"Delilah does but I was hoping you'd be able to answer that for me," he said, a grin in his voice.

"Then let's meet him. I'll share my impressions when he leaves."

"Perfect."

Once more, the sizzle of food in a pan – eggs this time – met Mia when they stood in Delilah's kitchen, where the old woman introduced Christopher.

"A pleasure to meet you, Mia," he said, the jingle of small bells accompanying his movement – presumably, he had stretched out his hand for her to shake.

She reached forth, judging from her memory of the sound, and found his grip. He wore rings on two fingers and bore the calluses of a sailor. "And you." So far, her gift offered no warning bells.

"So, you want to know about the *Angelique*?"

"Please," she said.

"Well, I've searched for it half my blasted life and I regret to say it probably doesn't exist – or if it does, it's hidden far more cunningly than I could fathom," he said. "Thought I came close once but I'm not sure I can afford another failure."

"What do you mean?" Ethan asked, and Mia heard a chair scrape back against the stone floor.

"West of Tamas there's a river mouth, hard rowing upstream. But two days inland you come to a mighty pool 'neath a waterfall and though we dived for hours and hours, we uncovered nothing but a chill that day."

"But something led you there, some clue or rumour. Something we might be able to use," Ethan said.

"That it did. A single entry in a diary found beneath the town hall here in Tamas – but it was a false trail or probably a false myth on the day the writer wrote it himself, decades ago now."

"Could we read it?" Mia asked.

"I probably still have a copy somewhere."

"No," Mia said, a little more forcefully than she intended. It *had* to be the original; it was just like the watch with the moon-face – her Gift was urging her toward the actual parchment... a leather-bound journal with a wine stain on the pages... and the symbol of Gatehouse on the cover. "I think the original would be better."

Christopher chuckled. "The words are the same, girl."

"There's something important in the original; I know it. Something you missed before, but we might find now."

"You know it, do you?" he asked, and this time he sounded doubtful rather than amused.

"Yes." Mia described the diary. "I am."

A moment of silence.

"Well, Christopher?" Ethan asked. "Do you have it?"

"No... wait. Young lady, how did you know? There's *no* way you could have seen it; you'd have been a child."

"Let's just say I have a gift," Mia said. "Now, what of the diary?"

"So be it," he said. "There's a fellow who collects stories about Tamas and the southern region. Calls himself an archivist; he has it."

"I'll send Javier," Delilah said.

"Wonderful," Mia said with a smile of her own.

More jingling from small bells now, and the thud of boots too, as Christopher began to pace, his silhouette moving back and forth before the window. "I can hardly believe it."

"Do your best, Captain," Mia said. "As I have a request."

"Captain? No longer, I run an inn now."

"Hmmm... well, we need someone with a ship and someone who knows the river mouth. You said it was unmarked?"

He did not answer at first, only the tinkling of his bells and Delilah's eggs sizzling followed her question. "Can't believe I'm saying this, but I wonder if we wouldn't succeed this time, with you along."

"Along?" Mia asked.

Ethan laughed, and even Delilah cackled from her chair. "Sounds like you're about to be hired, Christopher."

"So it does," he replied and now there was a clear trace of excitement in his voice. "Very well, I'll gather a crew. It'll take some wrangling but give me two days and I'll have everything we need."

Chapter 9

Thomas started down the long hallway, lamps guiding him toward a reinforced steel door with a heavy knocker shaped as a fist. His escort, another surly guard, had left Thomas to walk the last passage alone – due to laziness or by Elisabeth's design?

Yet he could not spare it much of a thought and his steps quickened. *You'll find out soon enough.* And more importantly, whether Mia was truly aboard the Sand-Hog. Whether Elisabeth was lying as she had so often in the past. *Like the lies she told about Leah – and who was ever going to take the word of two slaves over a noble?*

"Stay a moment, Thomas."

A purring voice echoed behind him.

Thomas spun. The corridor was empty... yet something moved in the shadows between lamps. Glittering eyes stared from the dark. A pale hand beckoned.

"Who are you?" Thomas demanded.

"You cannot be so dense."

The voice *was* familiar... Fox? Thomas took a single step forward and folded his arms. "Not going to come into the light for this conversation?"

"I think not, no."

"What orders from the false king, then?"

"Tut, tut – how very unseemly. Nevertheless, here it is – learn what you can of Alita's Shell."

"What is that?"

"Be subtle, mind." The sound of metal scraping against metal followed and then silence.

"Hey." Thomas stepped closer now, reaching up for a lamp. He unhooked it from its setting and shone light on the wall. A seamless bulkhead and panels of steel. No hint of a doorway or hatch but that was surely what it concealed. He knelt and ran his fingertips across the steel floor, faint scratch marks.

No way to follow.

And he's not my priority anyway. Not now – it doesn't matter what he wants. Or threatens. The truth about Mia came first. Thomas rose to replace the lamp then strode to Elisabeth's door and thumped on the surface.

The steel held but a minor indention was revealed when he stopped.

Good.

From beyond, the scrape of bolts sliding free and then Elisabeth opened the door. She smiled at him. "Come in and find a seat." She still wore her white shirt and dark leather pants, silver revolver at her hip. *Taking no chances, then.* She gestured with a gloved hand, to the dim room. A lamp-lit table arranged with steaming meats, vegetables and blood-coloured wine. Two servants – or slaves – were leaving the room, one wheeling a trolley. Vague shapes only lurked beyond the light, shelving and a rifle stand, a second and third door perhaps.

Two places had been set at the table and the rich scent of gravy reached him where he stood; beef, too, and vegetables – a far cry from the dried fruit, bread, and water he'd been afforded in his cell.

"Where is Mia?"

"Sit and I will tell you," Elisabeth instructed as she closed the door behind him, then gave him a shove.

He found a chair then crossed his arms. *I am a fool.* "Where?"

Elisabeth took her own seat and lifted a glass of wine, inhaling a moment then setting it down without drinking. "Do you know much about the history of our sorry nation, Thomas?"

He stood and pointed across the table. "I was an idiot to swallow your lies, obvious as they were, Elisabeth, but hear me now. One more and I will kill you, no matter the cost."

Now she did drink, green eyes watching him.

He glared back.

"You wanted to believe," she said with a shrug. "Don't judge yourself so harshly."

Thomas pushed his chair aside and started for the door. "I suddenly miss the comforts of my cell."

"Stop."

Elisabeth stood with her gun levelled at his face. Doubtless not a wound he'd recover from if she pulled the trigger.

"What now?"

"You think I have nothing to offer but that's wrong, Thomas. I can offer you your freedom, true freedom. From slavery, from Williams, from this entire pitiful continent for that matter."

"My freedom?" Thomas narrowed his eyes.

"If you help me willingly with my detour, yes – and I think you'll find it's something well within your specialised abilities."

"This won't work, either. For you to make that offer, you need to have credibility. And you have none."

Elisabeth approached, keeping the gun trained on his chest now as she slid to a halt directly before him. She raised an eyebrow as she leaned in. "I'm not saying you have to trust me – only that we could help each other and that it might even be quite... pleasant."

Thomas blinked. *What in all the hells was happening?*

"Just take a moment for yourself, Thomas. Freedom *from the entire nation*." Elisabeth ran her free hand across his cheek. His pulse tripled at her touch.

Madness.

How long had he loathed Elisabeth? How long had she hunted him, an ever-present threat hanging over his every move? The torment and lies from our youth. Her lies about Mia now. *She is an enemy*. Yet his treacherous body was reacting to her. Up close, the scent of rose from her hair was very welcome; her beauty now unmarred by the typical arrogance she displayed and her lips...

Thomas reached up and closed his fingers over the gun barrel.

"I am not that easy to manipulate."

"If you say so, Thomas." She smiled.

"I do."

Elisabeth stepped back, and Thomas released the weapon. "Off you go then."

She returned to the table and took her seat, exchanging

gun for fork and jabbing at a slab of meat. Gravy slid down the piece, dripping onto her plate. "Think about my offer while you're in that cell."

"You have my answer."

"Hurry along to the end of the passage and someone will escort you the rest of the way." She was still heaping food onto her plate; she'd started on the potatoes.

His gut seemed to gnash itself as he turned for the door.

Chapter 10

He had scratched fourteen tiny lines on the steel beside his cot; one for each meal of bread, water and the occasional fruit – seven days now since he'd made it clear to Elisabeth what he thought of her treachery.

Yet she'd lived in his dreams; his mind was plagued with thoughts of her. What did she want from him? How would it feel to lie with a woman again after so many years? Could she truly escape Williams? Escape the very land itself? Did she know something about the *Clara*? Or Aiden – the possibility of news on a pilot? If he went to her bed how long could he stay? How soft her skin?

And how much more power would she exert over him if he tangled himself in her web?

By all that is holy why do I find her attractive now, when every part of me hates her? He ran a hand through his hair where he lay. *Be honest, idiot.* It wasn't 'every' part of him that was a concern – it was a very specific part that was causing so much trouble.

By the time the dreams faded he was usually able to

recall that very obvious fact.

Of all the fears and desires that he could not shake was a single thought – how could he possibly betray Mia?

She suffered by Elisabeth's hand as much as me. And sleeping with Elisabeth won't get me a single step closer to finding Mia. Not in any way.

Nor would it, despite Elisabeth's claim, grant him freedom. Whatever she wanted from him would only make everything worse, likely for a lot of innocent people. All her promises were poison.

The muted rumble of the Sand-Hog eased.

Soon after, it came to a halt. Thomas threw his blanket aside and stood, listening with eyes closed. Time in his cell still allowed him to focus on his surroundings, to continue practicing how to respond to the mass of steel and iron that was the Sand-Hog – enough that he could sense the boilers easing, slowly, slowly cooling, the treads clanking, and doors slamming open, gun turrets swivelling for what he assumed was occasional firing practice.

Now, it seemed the Hog was coming to a complete halt, which suggested a settlement or watering hole at the least.

Yet it was the chains he'd spent most time focusing on.

There was a pattern beneath the impenetrable shielding, to whatever Silas had done to the steel. And today, Thomas would break it and win his freedom. If the Hog had stopped, it likely meant civilisation, which meant transportation.

If he had to rip, tear, and burrow his way from the Sand-Hog he'd do it; he had to take whatever tiny chance he'd been offered. The very real possibility that there was no town, no transportation and no chance of actually outrunning the Hog after, had to be confronted.

But only once he was free.

He lifted his bindings. The steel seemed alive; a cold, dark blue that somehow contrasted the walls around him. Because it was not wholly steel.

Not once had he come even close to breaking it with his strength.

Previously, when he'd tried to summon warmth, like he had in the past, to bend the chain, the friction he built had no effect and he'd given up, worn out and frustrated. Yet last night, it seemed there'd been something of a change, but Thomas had been interrupted by a guard with food.

He tried again now, using the blanket to prevent blistering, until the chain grew warm enough that the sense of whatever foreign material Silas had introduced returned. Mixed within the steel he sensed something, like thin green threads of vibrant twine.

They faded as he eased off. "No."

Thomas kept up the friction and willed the chain to break, continuing to apply heat, and it seemed the steel expanded a tiny amount... then the green twine snapped down harder, as if responding aggressively to his actions.

He let the chains drop with a clank. "Bastard."

Footsteps echoed, growing louder. They stopped at his door, which soon opened to reveal Sergeant Wilkins and his sweeping moustache. A second soldier, a younger fellow, stood with him.

"Lady Elisabeth needs you for this," the sergeant said.

Thomas stood. "Why?"

"I imagine she'll explain why soon enough," Wilkins said, waving his subordinate into the room.

Once free of his shackle, Thomas followed them through

the shadowy interior and to the upper floors, where more men were striding about, checking weapons or wrenching levers to drop heavy shutters over the windows.

Topside, the afternoon sun was sinking, tinting the surrounds a warm yellow; it gleamed on the rifle barrels and the Gatling guns. Soldiers lined the rails, and Elisabeth stood there too, nearer the front of the decking. She was shading her face as she stared across the sands, spyglass held to one eye.

Wilkins dismissed his subordinate then led Thomas to where she stood.

"My lady."

"Excellent." She waved Thomas closer without turning. "Tell me what you see out there?"

Thomas squinted. The red sand stretched, eddies of wind twirling as they raced across sloping dunes, the occasional thin tree visible. This far west, further than he'd ever travelled, seemed little different than the northern desert but there was a distinctive feature, a rocky sort of funnel that led between two ridges.

The dunes levelled off before it, enough for Thomas to see small shapes... a ruined merchant train? Yes, wagons and camels lay in a twisted heap. No movement, either.

"Bandits?" he asked. Even as he spoke, the suggestion seemed unlikely – where would such a camp even exist out here?

"No. Something much worse – wait, and you will see it."

So wait he did.

And for a time, nothing stirred. Then a small head appeared above a dune – a camel, riderless. A blanket trailed from the animal's saddle and it was tossing its head as it ran.

"There, the last one. Watch," Elisabeth said.

The animal had barely made it halfway down the slope when sand exploded around it; flinging the poor creature into the air. Within the wall of sand, something dark and mammoth lurked – but in glimpses only.

Thomas gripped the steel beneath his hands, warping it almost without realising. *That thing has to be half again the size of the Sand-Hog!* The camel hit the dune and rolled to a halt – soundless at such a distance – half-covered by still-falling sand. A black shape, a head with a gaping maw visible even from a distance rose next, sand pouring from its ridges as it nudged the corpse. Then, a cloud of black steam poured forth, engulfing the camel.

Cries of horror echoed from the men who'd obviously not seen the creature yet and when the black cloud was sucked back within the thing, revealing pure white bones, Thomas nearly joined them.

"What is it?" he breathed as the creature slithered toward the wreckage and heaved itself onto the harder ground, where once more, its inky cloud poured forth. Behind the gargantuan beast, the sand stirred as its body followed, a vaguely sinuous shape. A jagged, spiked tail flicked from the dune at a point at least thirty feet behind the beast as it... feasted.

"Have you not heard stories of the Blighted Ones?"

He had. Supposedly malformed, mythical beasts left behind after some vast calamity that rocked the entire world, wiping the very earth clean with unholy fire and poisoning much of what survived for generations. David had once called them the Lean Eons, whatever that meant. Yet it could hardly be true, could it? "You think that creature is one such thing?"

She handed him the eye-glass. "You tell me."

Thomas lifted the lens to his eye and roamed across the red sand until he found the thing's mottled body – a worm-like row of folded skin, grey and black. Even as he noted the apparent decay; a hunk of flesh dropped to the dune. The back of its head was a misshapen row of twisted ridges... which was probably a blessing. *How can we avoid such a thing?*

"We have to turn back," he said.

Elisabeth smiled. "Very prudent, of course, but that's not going to happen."

"You can get you and your own men killed if you want, but I won't be a part of it."

She sighed. "So eager to pick a fight. Take just a moment to think, Thomas. Look around."

"I don't have to – I know we're probably days from any water or towns, but I don't care. I'll take my chances in the desert."

"You won't have to."

"Think the Hog can outrun that thing?"

"No. But we need to pass along that road."

Thomas folded his arms. "Go around."

"You've never been to the Inland Federation, have you?" Wilkins asked.

"No."

"There's a series of gorges beyond. Trails between them are too narrow for the tread," he explained. "And a detour would cost us too much water; we have to reach the Katadar Oasis by tomorrow."

Thomas shook his head. "Do you really think you can take it on?"

"We have no choice," Elisabeth said. "In the end, it's that simple."

Chapter 11

"So what's your plan?" Thomas asked.

The blightworm, as he had already begun to think of it, was still feasting but would finish soon enough. Guessing its next move wasn't difficult. It would either retreat to its lair, or at least *seem* to do so, then lie in wait for the Hog's approach or simply turn and attack. There was no conceivable way it wasn't aware of the Sand-Hog.

Damn this, I can think of far less horrendous ways to die.

Not that death was an option. *I have to find Mia. And Ethan.*

"To make the first move," Elisabeth said. "Strike while it's busy eating; we should get a few good shots in before it turns on us."

"Assuming your canons can even hurt that thing," Thomas said.

"You saw its hide. I'll wager my entire family fortune on us." She glanced at him. "You going to help? Or do I send you back to your cell?"

He shook his head. Better to die fighting than shackled

in a cell... and maybe there'd be a chance to escape too. "Fine. I want the biggest gun you have."

Wilkins slapped Thomas on the back. "Good man. I'll get you something special; palace has been working on this since the day you disappeared. I'd love to see it in action with a real target."

"Very well."

Elisabeth laughed as she started for a doorway beneath the main turret. Wilkins took Thomas to a different door, then along a wide passage teeming with grim-faced men, heading deeper into the centre of the Hog until they reached a heavily-reinforced door that stood ajar – a large symbol of a bullet engraved there.

As Wilkins spoke with one of the black-clad men who came to meet the sergeant, Elisabeth's voice rang out – it seemed some manner of speaking tube had been placed within the armoury, as her voice was quite clear compared to the muffled tones that obviously blasted from the outside.

"Take up battle positions. After a frontal assault, we'll attempt to strafe the worm. If it ends up being your side, I want full fire concentrated on its head. The rest of you, hold in case it slips around or beneath us. On my signal, and *only* my signal, I want all firepower from all hands on the Blighted One." A pause. "This is a gamble, you all know that – but you also know I've never let anything stop me before. This worm will be no different."

A cheer echoed around him, but Thomas couldn't stop a snort. *This is no time for bravado.*

"Thomas." Wilkins gestured him closer. A pair of men were carrying something from the armoury, their faces showing some strain. The weapon had a four-foot barrel with a wide mouth; it looked as though it could tear through a wall. A handle had been attached beneath the shaft and a steel plate too, presumably to be connected to a stand of some sort – a guess confirmed when a third soldier appeared carrying just such an item.

"It fires heavy ten-pound shot so the recoil is far too much for a normal man," Wilkins explained. "You'll need to make sure it doesn't knock you off your feet."

A normal man? Thomas glanced around. "Is there a boiler coming? Or does it use gunpowder?"

"Powder – it's not as elegant as a rifle; there's a match set up to strike when you pull a piece of rope."

A fourth fellow brought up a crate of iron balls and set it down with a grunt.

"I'm risking my life by using this."

"Well, The Alchemist didn't think you'd have any trouble," Wilkins said, smoothing his moustache. "And it worked well enough on the first trial – we've already reinforced the stand."

"And I load the powder?"

One of the soldiers unhooked a modest-looking keg from his belt. "Should be enough for at least a dozen shots."

A rumbling from deep within the Hog grew.

The sergeant raised his voice. "Get moving."

Thomas lifted the canon; heavy enough but nothing he couldn't handle, then slung it over one shoulder. "Find me some rope for that crate and tie it so I can carry the damn thing."

One of the soldiers muttered to himself but still complied, wrapping the rope around four ways, then tying a knot. Thomas lifted it and paused while Wilkins tied the keg of powder to Thomas' belt. "Percy, follow him with the stand," the sergeant instructed.

"Yes, Sergeant."

Once again, Wilkins led the way back up and to battle positions. The Hog was churning sand now as it moved. Soldiers were still setting up – men with magnifiers positioned higher, around Elisabeth's dome; men with twin-shot beside those arming the silent Gatlings. Most faces were tight, though a few men seemed exhilarated, whooping and hurling insults into the wind.

Some glanced at Thomas as he passed, but most were focused on the target – which, as Thomas stopped to set his weapon down, seemed to have already finished its meal. The thing was turning to face the approaching Hog. They were still a fair distance away, but the worm reared up, weaving like a cobra.

This is true madness.

Steel squeaked nearby.

Percy was spreading the stand, its bulky legs split into a tripod, a heavy connecting plate atop. "Slide the plates together then pull this lever to lock them in place," the man said, then ran off.

Thomas lifted the cannon and fitted it in place. It slid home easily with a clank that he barely registered over the din around him. Once on the stand, the weapon moved easily. Thomas opened the crate and dumped the first iron ball within. *How many chances will I even get to load this thing?*

He bent over the handle; a small piece of rope rested alongside, ready to fire. He ran his hands across the barrel and found a tiny hatch nearby. A gust of grey powder puffed free, so he closed it, but that was enough – there was a place for a match to lock in place. Now, hopefully, he had matches too.

"In the keg," a voice said.

Elisabeth stood beside him, shielding her eyes against the sun with a gloved hand; he hadn't heard her approach.

"Not planning to hide out in your dome, then."

"This is where the action is, Thomas," she said, ignoring his barb.

"Right." Thomas opened the keg's lid. A tiny cloth bag lay upon the powder – within were two dozen matches at least. "Do you really think we have a chance against this thing?"

She pointed. "So long as that tail doesn't knock us over. And the Hog weighs *many* tonnes, Thomas. So I doubt it will."

"And its breath or whatever it used to melt that camel?"

"That's probably more troubling." She leant closer with a nod. "Don't break Silas' toy by the way."

A boom from the main turret rocked the deck, cutting off Thomas' reply. It shot across the space between Hog and worm, landing just wide, a red cloud following. The worm flinched, then surged forward, sand spraying into the air.

"Again!" Elisabeth roared up at them.

Doubtless they were already re-loading because a second shot was not far behind, this struck the beast as it swerved, rolling the worm off course. A shrill screech echoed across the dunes, answered by a cheer from the men, but there was something deeply unpleasant about the creature's cry and he shivered.

The Hog altered its path, nearing steadily; it gave the soldiers on Thomas' side a chance to attack, and their first clear look at the blightworm. As he'd judged from a distance, it was colossal – taller than the Hog and probably three times as long. It thrashed, sand swirling, but the glimpses he caught were enough. The skin was a grey and black mess, pieces flaking free to reveal rotting flesh as the worm turned, its head remaining, for now, lost in the sand.

Gunfire exploded in a deafening roar as the main turret fired a third time and every man, whether he held twin-shot or Gatling, joined in. Thomas swung his barrel and ripped the rope free – and nothing happened. "Bastard," he cried.

The Hog was already turning for a second pass and Elisabeth was amongst her men, offering praise and bolstering them for the next attack. A huge burst of steam shot from the stacks as the Hog laboured to turn such a sharp arc.

Yet the worm was moving again.

It surged forward, too fast for the Hog. Another blast from the main and secondary steam canons flew off mark as the worm dipped below the sand. Thomas scrambled for another match, swearing as he fumbled with the drawstring.

Finally, he had a match; he ripped open the hatch and set it in place, then got a good grip on the weapon.

Gunfire rang out from the rear, opposite Thomas' position. A column of sand spurted forth, falling across the Hog.

Thomas flinched.

The worm's maw was clearly visible when it reared up. Dead, black eyes, each the size of a man's torso, sat above and to the side of the mouth, which was lined with pulsing sacs. Bullets pummelled into the worm and it seemed to draw in a breath as it twisted out of his line of vision.

"Turn!" Thomas screamed.

The Hog was too slow – a vast acidic hiss rang out, followed instantly by screams that were cut short. The Sand-Hog continued to change direction, whether the engineers had heard Thomas or not.

More fire from rifles and cracking shots from the secondary steam canon followed, joined by the Gatlings' continued rasping growl.

"Where is it?" someone cried.

Something swirled beneath the sand, tips of sharp spikes just visible. Thomas braced himself, but the tail did not attack. The Sand-Hog was picking up speed, heading for the stony ground near the path between peaks. *Where the worm won't be as dexterous perhaps.*

Shouts of alarm came from the rear of the Hog.

Thomas lifted his canon, stand and all, and started to the rear. "Someone bring that ammunition," he called.

Footsteps thundered after him.

"Make room," Thomas shouted as he ran, descending a short flight of stairs that ran beneath portholes, weapons protruding. Sweat was building, running down his neck and back, slicking his hands, but once more his fingers made slight grooves in the steel, ensuring the canon remained easy to hold.

Up a second flight of steel steps and he found himself on the rear deck, where immediately to his left the scent of sulphur presided over a blackened and twisted rail. Small heaps that were once men rested around holes like pockmarks in the decking.

Injured soldiers were huddled against the walls in their tattered flak jackets, skin red and raw. Other survivors still manned the remaining weapons, pumping round after round into the trailing worm, their shouts lost in the chaos.

Thomas set his weapon at an empty space beside one of the gunners. Then he glanced behind him, the soldier carrying the crate was nearing.

"Sorry," the man said as he dumped the gear, chest heaving.

The main canon boomed overhead, the iron punching through the creature's body, disappearing soundlessly. Yet the worm screeched once more – Thomas clamped his hands over his ears.

When Thomas could hear once more, he braced himself, leaning slightly in to the weapon, and tore the rope free.

A flash of light and smoke blinded him. The recoil drove the cannon back into his chest – yet he absorbed the blow, the pain washing over him, only half-realised. The worm screeched again; the ball had splattered its way through an eye.

"Another," he cried as he lifted the canon.

The soldier heaved a ball to Thomas, which he dumped into the barrel. Then he righted the weapon, tore open the hatch and dumped a fistful of powder within. "I need a match."

The main canon fired again.

Once more, the worm's shrill cry of pain split the air.

Thomas fitted the match in place then snapped the hatch closed. He swung the barrel around, aiming for the head. The worm was straining to reach the Sand-Hog now, black mist streaming from its mouth, whipped away by the wind garnered from its own speed.

He wrenched the rope down.

Another flash. He blinked his vision clear; the shot cut through the worm's mouth, bursting one of the sacs before punching out through the other side of its head. The main turret fired again, striking out another eye, exploding through from a slightly different angle.

The blightworm did not scream – it faltered now.

It slowed, twitching as its head drooped toward the ground. Its whole body seemed caught in a furious shiver. Dark sand leapt and swirled as it crashed to a halt, rolling and spinning, the massive body bearing down on the Sand-Hog.

Thomas fell back, the soldiers around him following his example, guns falling silent.

Only the roar of the engines remained then.

The worm was still tumbling closer when the entire Hog jolted. Thomas gripped the wall – had they hit harder earth already? The Sand-Hog continued forward. *It's going to work.* The stony earth gripped, snagged, and tore at the worm's body, spewing chunks of rotting flesh. The Sand-Hog drew away, soon slowing to curve around and stop some distance from the thing.

A torn curtain of red sand drifted from the body, which remained motionless.

Thomas straightened.

Around him, men were moving to the rail or rising to their feet, cautious hope in their expressions.

And then a lone cheer rose, joined swiftly by the entire crew of the Sand-Hog.

Chapter 12

Birds called from the trees, shrill compared to the flapping of the mainsail or the grunting of the crew as they worked the oars. Christopher's ship, the *Fleet*, was a trireme; it bore a dozen oars and a score of men to work them in shifts, not including the captain and Ethan, who each took a turn.

Whenever Ethan returned it was with a somewhat more ginger step, but he never complained to her, where she sat in the stern, a little ways from the tillerman who hummed as he worked, not that he seemed to have much to do; the river was broad, according to the captain and Ethan, and few obstacles presented themselves.

"Switch," a voice hollered, and shuffling feet and cursing followed.

Soon enough, Ethan approached, his outline clear but more than that – the sense of him had grown so much stronger, more familiar over the course of their search. It was like an imprint upon her mind that made him instantly recognisable, like Thomas. Or David – or even Julian and

Williams and Elisabeth.

"Thinking of Thomas?" Ethan asked as he stopped nearby, probably leaning against the rail.

"I suppose I was," she said. A slight headache didn't help but it was far more than that.

"I thought so – you have that pensive look again."

"This is still the right choice... but it's hard. I can't help worrying anyway. He still has to deal with Elisabeth."

"He's strong, Mia; it runs in the family."

She tilted her head to the sound of his voice. It was as though he still faced away, toward the water. "Thank you." Maybe she could recognise him swiftly enough but reading Ethan lately was becoming more difficult. Was he trying to allay her fears or pay her a compliment? Both? *Maybe it's you, maybe* you're *the one who's changed – you're letting your thoughts run wild about everything now.*

Ever since the misunderstanding with the rooms.

Or earlier than that.

Delilah simply brought something to the fore, something she'd been holding back from admitting – the risk was too great. Wasn't it? *After the way Elisabeth set me up for one. Or the boy; Thomas beat him to a pulp. Henry.* He'd been a slave too... rough, cruel.

And stupid.

"Have you had any more visions about the pilot? The one that corpse thinks we're supposed to make."

"I'm sure the dead meant 'teach' but no, nothing else so far."

"What about the journal?"

"Not yet." She lifted the leather-bound book from where it sat in her lap; tracing the hourglass symbol on the cover with her fingertips. The keyhole within the centre had been engraved like the rest of the design, edges rough. Ethan had read her each page and while it proved a compelling account of Gatehouse's activities in the south, and while it also mentioned both the *Clara* and other airships in addition to the *Angelique*, the sense that she'd still missed something lingered. "Would you read me the entry that mentions Stella, again?" She held the book out to him.

"Near the back, wasn't it?" The dry rustle of pages being turned came next and then Ethan cleared his throat. "Here it is. 'Stella has changed, despite our many victories – something troubles her. I have not seen her smile since we left Alita's Shell.' The next paragraph talks about the raid on Viterra."

"Hmmm. What about the defeat at sea?"

More pages turning. "Right. Which part?"

"Just the aftermath," Mia said. "I thought there was something about the wreck that seemed odd."

"How about this: 'We considered trying to salvage both equipment and bodies but Williams' and his blasted warships patrol too often. Perhaps if we could contact the *Eva* but something is jamming our radio. We will have to fall back inland but I fear God will judge us harshly for abandoning our comrades. So much is lost, their lives yes, but pieces of our future too. The powerful gifts from the mountain-folk... we will feel their loss most keenly but at least I have managed to hide the Mist of Dawn as we all agreed – let no thieving Dirt King touch it.' Do you recognise any of that? The Mist of Dawn? And who are the mountain-folk and their gifts?"

Mia shook her head. "No. I thought something might

come to me but none of it is familiar – including Alita's Shell. They all seem important at least."

"Well, what about the *Angelique*? Christopher says we'll reach the lake by noon – do you want to check that page again?"

"We should." Christopher had already explained what the journal claimed, that the *Angelique* was at the mouth of a waterfall but that he and his men had searched for days, diving the pool and examining the Saridaw Falls all for naught.

"It says: 'The *Angelique* is in need of repair; it only just reached the falls. It will take some time, but I like it here, the song of the honeyeaters is pleasant and the pool is like a tiny lake, perfect for swimming. Perhaps I will ask Magdalena to marry me tomorrow. I have certainly put it off too long and who knows what the future holds'."

Had they married? There was no way to know. *I hope they did.* "I'm struck once more by the level of organisation," she said.

"Exactly. You'd think there would be some trace, especially if they were repairing an entire ship."

"But there's no more clues in the passage," Mia said with a sigh. "After the twentieth time hearing it, I feel like we should have figured it out by now."

"Maybe the answer lies at the falls themselves and we won't know until we're there."

"I hope so," Mia said. "Because I fear we're running out of options."

***

The Saridaw Falls roared where Mia stood on the banks beside Ethan and Christopher, the thud of hammers against wood nearly muted by the churn of the water. The men were racing the dying sun to finish building diving platforms – rafts, truly – which would be launched from the ship where it had anchored off the centre of the pool.

From Ethan's description, it wasn't truly a small lake, more a vast pool whose waters were dark and deep. "Pale leaves from ghost gums collect at the edge of the water and the waterfall leaps from the dark hills. There's a rock shelf that looks like it might lead behind the fall too – it's a pretty spot."

"If it wasn't so far from Tamas I could imagine building a cabin here for when I grow old," Christopher added.

"Let's see if we can find something this time," Mia said. "We should start with the waterfall."

"I'll manage the diving then," Christopher said. "At least three of the men here were with me on the last trip; we'll see what they remember."

"Allow me, Mia," Ethan said. "The footing will be quite slippery up there."

Without her rifle, and due to the truth of his words, it was safer to have him guide her but for just a fraction she hesitated before reaching out. His hand found hers, skin warm and grip firm – a welcome comfort, and not just in a practical sense.

Together they walked around the shore, the crash of water growing louder as they climbed, Ethan leading and describing the immediate terrain. At one point he stopped. The sound of falling water suggested a short drop to the pool below, but the thought of tumbling down into the river still caused a certain tension in her muscles. "I have to let go a moment – there's a big step we need to take. I'll catch you from the other side."

"Right." Mia stepped back, keeping one hand against the shadowed rock face.

Stone scraped, followed by a thud. "Done. Now you – half a step and you'll feel the edge. It's not much of a leap but a big step."

She crept forward with a frown. Jumping without knowing when or where she'd land was never easy. "Does the way curve or dip?"

"Straight and even."

"Try and warn me so I can judge the landing."

"How?"

"Just talk," Mia said. She kept one hand against the wall, bent her legs and leapt forward. Air rushed across her face – as if she were falling suddenly – but Ethan's voice, raised to compete with the falls, gave her something to orient herself with. Her feet smacked onto stone and she stumbled but Ethan caught her around the waist.

"Nicely done," he said as he released her.

Had his grip lingered a little? Mia exhaled heavily. "I'm not looking forward to doing that again."

"If we're really lucky we can sail back down the river."

"Only if we get inside – is there much behind the water?"

"Let's see."

Ethan led Mia once more, the spray from the fall dampening one side of her body. She wiped at her face with her free hand then came to a halt when Ethan stopped, once more raising his voice. "The stone is rough, I can't see tool marks or any hint of a door but if it were here somehow, it'd lead to a big cavern."

"We're in the right place," Mia said. "I feel it."

"Any ideas of how to get inside?"

"Not yet but being here... the past seems very close, somehow." She stepped forward, hands outstretched until her fingers brushed the wall. She pressed her palms against the cool stone, letting the words from the journal echo in her mind.

A giant hourglass with a shattered keyhole appeared – the vision pulsed and faded quickly. *Maybe luck is on our side after all; Thomas would have agreed.*

"Let's return to the others – there must be a way to open this," she said.

"In the pool?"

"Or on the banks nearby? Something is hidden somewhere, that much I know."

"Then we should search from the opposite side to that where we entered. It might be an easier path back down too."

"I'd welcome that."

Once more, Ethan took her hand and led her in an examination of what did turn out to be another path back down to the others, though it placed them on the opposite side to Christopher's camp. Still, he sent one of the men, Stephen, across to them.

Water trickled to the grass as the man splashed from the pool. "So, we've found something – the same stone shapes I came across last time," he said, and she caught the suggestion of an accent. An Inland Federation man? "Maybe you'll know what they mean."

"Can you describe them?"

"Not well. It's too dark down there to see anything but I can feel four or five squares that might be protruding from something important, or maybe something just fell down there one time," he said. "I think there might be more shapes because there's a build-up of silt down there that's probably clogging the space between others."

"Is there anything else about them?" Ethan asked.

"Hard to say. Last time we ignored them because there are other rocks and stone pieces too and none of them turned out to be anything. We were blind down there anyway," he said, then mumbled an apology to Mia, his tone becoming mortified.

"It's fine, Stephen. Tell me why those stones caught your interest?"

"They're just quite regular, as though they've been cut to shape – I don't know what to do with them, they don't seem to move. If I could just see, maybe I'd figure out a pattern or something."

Mia pursed her lips. "What if I could give you more light?"

"You carry around a second sun in your pocket?"

"Almost," she said with a grin. "Head back to your raft and tell Christopher I'm going to handle the light."

"If you say so."

"Trust me," she said. "And I don't know how much time you'll have, so maybe two of you should head down to see as much as possible."

"Will do, my lady," he said over new splashing.

"The Bird of Light?" Ethan asked.

"I hope so." Mia stretched her arms up to the sky and closed her eyes, whispering the lullaby to herself.

"Dramatic," Ethan said.

"Shut-up, Ethan."

"Yes ma'am."

Mia smiled but let it fade as she lifted her voice, the lullaby growing louder. From the opposite shore curious chatter rose but she let the sounds wash over her, unheard. Even Ethan's calm presence beside her faded as she let the words ring out, louder and louder.

Please, Great One, I need you now.

A glittering comet of golden, brilliant light filled her mind and she cried out in joy. Echoing shouts came from all around; the ship, the rafts and the banks, shock, fear and awe all mixed in but they soon fell away to a reverent hush as the Bird of Light settled on the ships' mainmast, sending its incandescent rays spearing into the water.

The bird knew not to blind anyone; none of the sailors cried out in despair. The magnificent creature knew not to burn them too, not to strike terror into their hearts, by the silence it spread, choosing not to use its piercing cry – all without Mia giving any such direction.

Are you a Goddess?

It did not answer but twin splashes followed.

Mia found herself holding her breath; she even took a step toward the bird in her eagerness. A gentle hand on her shoulder kept her from going too far and she murmured her thanks.

After what seemed an eternity, far too long for anyone to hold their breath, surely, more splashing echoed across the pool as Stephen and the second diver broke the surface.

"It's easier to make out now – there's eleven squares, not five," Stephen called to her.

"And they can move," the other man added. "We cleaned the gunk and they slid around."

"Make an hourglass," Mia called.

"What do you mean?" Stephen replied.

"Arrange them into lines. Three at the top, then two in the next line and one in the middle. It's two and then three for the very bottom – you'll see it."

"Right."

"Are you sure about this?" Ethan asked.

"Yes. It's an obvious symbol for Gatehouse to use as a lock, I know – but it's not in an obvious place."

"True. And we'll find out soon enough."

Time dragged, like two snails racing, but when the water finally broke again Stephen called at once. "Did anything happen?"

"No," Mia called back. But there was something else to attempt; the answer drifted across the dark of her vision. "Try something else for me."

"Of course."

"Push on the middle square; it'll collapse."

"Back in a flash," he said.

Mia turned her face to the waterfall where it crashed down behind the Great Bird, and waited. It was only a matter of moments now, she knew it – the '*something*' reassured her. Whether it was her gift or the bird, it didn't matter.

And then a rumbling echoed across the pool.

"You did it," Ethan cried.

"Not without help," Mia replied, and even as she spoke, the Bird of Light began to fade. *Thank you, Great One.*

Chapter 13

Mia stood within the cavern, a chill settling across her shoulders – a chill that seemed to come from more than just the deepening of night. The crackle of nearby torches and the creak of lantern handles were audible over the distant waterfall, where it continued to plunge into the pool beyond the opening – a stone wall that had left behind fragments of rock and dust as it rose into the hill.

"What do you see?" she asked.

"Nothing," Ethan said, his voice barely a whisper.

"Search the whole thing," Christopher growled. "There must be another door."

Mia fumbled for Ethan's arm. "What's wrong? I don't sense anything amiss."

He took her hand. "We're standing in a large cavern, easily enough to hold a great steamship such as the *Angelique* was said to be, but it is empty. There's a great pool of water here too..." he paused. "And along the walls, crates and canvas coverings but no ship."

Mia swallowed. "No sign of it?" *How? I found a way*

in. The diary claimed that she had taken repairs here... Has Williams been here before? Or the remnants of Gatehouse? "I don't feel the kind of emptiness that would suggest we failed. It doesn't make sense."

"Perhaps it was once here," Ethan said.

"I suppose."

"Come and see this, you two," a voice called. Christopher. There was excitement and awe in his words once more.

She kept a hand on Ethan's shoulder as she followed the clack of his boots across even ground, slowing when he did – it seemed they were now near the crates.

"There's all kinds of supplies here; copper piping, steel sheets, rivets and weapons too." He paused to take a breath. "And two strongboxes worth of silver; it's a small fortune."

"What else?" Mia asked.

Christopher chuckled. "You deserve your share of the loot, Mia – without you, we wouldn't be here."

"I trust you to be fair with my and Ethan's share, Captain," she said.

"Most certainly."

"And you wanted us to see all of this?" Ethan asked.

A hinge squeaked. "And this."

Ethan gave a low whistle. "If that is genuine..."

"Considering where we've just found it, it must be, surely."

"What is it?" Mia asked, a touch of impatience in her voice.

"A bottle of wine – it's over two hundred years old," Ethan replied.

"From the Golden Lakes Vineyard," Christopher added. "Might just be the rarest vintage ever."

"Wonderful – anything else in th..." she trailed off.

The bottle was the reason they'd found the cavern – not the missing *Angelique.*

"Mia?"

"Check the label," she said. "There's something we need to know, some piece of information we need." *You cannot find a pilot; you must make one.* The words of the corpse echoed in her head, a chill joining them.

"What am I looking for?" Christopher asked.

"Tell me what you see; I'll know when I hear it."

"Well then... the label's yellowed with age but the glue ain't weakened yet. The lettering's like a quill, ah, picture of a lake covered in leaves – I'm supposing they're meant to be yellow but it's black ink. There's a hotel or might be a restaurant on the edge."

As he spoke, a vision fell over Mia; a tranquil lake whose dark surface lay littered with green and gold leaves. At the opposite end stood a vineyard, stone buildings of the winery itself, along with what looked like a considerable glasshouse converted into a dining hall. A wooden deck extended onto the lake; upon it tables had been set for a meal, nobles in their finery sat amongst them, laughing as they ate. Slaves moved between the benches, balancing trays of blood-coloured wine.

And all of it appearing as if set behind a screen of watery, wavering lines.

"Does the restaurant look like a glasshouse?"

"Aye."

"We need to go there, Ethan," Mia said.

"Are you sure?"

"Very. I don't know why, but more answers are waiting there."

Christopher clapped his hands together. "Then let me take you. There's a beach you can land upon, then strike out inland. You'd have to cross the ruins of Aderlen but it shouldn't take more than a few days on foot to reach Golden Lakes."

"Then that's what we'll have to do," Mia said. "We can prepare back at Delilah's."

"Just let us round up the loot and we'll head back," the captain said.

Ethan took Mia out and past the waterfall, using the easier path once more. On the great pool's shore they signalled to the *Fleet*, and someone soon started their way, using long poles to push a raft.

"Do you want to give up on the *Albion* for now?" Ethan asked as they waited.

"Maybe not totally... but our efforts haven't borne much in the way of fruit, have they?"

"No. We still might be able to circle further west to check the ports there and continue north. Aiden will have to come back to Silver Rock sooner or later; he won't be able to resist the jewel mine. We could wait there."

"I agree, but we could be waiting a long time."

"True."

"Perhaps while my visions are leading me toward Gatehouse – or at least, in another direction, I feel we should trust them."

"Let's see where they take us," Ethan agreed. "Even without the *Angelique*, this has still been an amazing find. Golden Lakes may have something better waiting for us."

"Thank you, Ethan," she said.

"For what?"

She turned to face his silhouette. "For believing in me."

"Do you doubt yourself?" His tone suggested surprise. "You seemed certain in the cavern."

"I am... but I still feel less alone with your support."

"Oh."

He seemed about to add more but a voice interrupted; Stephen, calling from the raft. "I hope Captain's saving some of the treasure for his star diver."

"So long as it doesn't come out of our share," Ethan called back.

"*Your* share? Hah! Don't you mean Mia's share?"

Ethan laughed. "Fine – you and Christopher can split whatever's left after she's done, how does that sound?"

"Sounds fair to me."

Mia had to smile.

Chapter 14

The Sand-Hog rumbled to a halt before the blightworm, the mighty plow at its nose nudging the body.

Groans and coughing came from soldiers gathered on the decking; a dry, acrid stench lingered in the air. Some of the smell seemed to seep from the mottled body, its decaying surface uneven, but most of the scent drifted over from the nearby head.

It lay open, tilted to the side.

Black blood poured from dozens of wounds – some gaping holes – that littered the face, neck, and head. One of the shots must have pierced the brain… if it had one. Most of the men seemed to credit this to Thomas, though he felt more certain it was the main turret, and said so.

Still, he was earning a few less scowls than before.

"I don't think this is a good idea, my lady," Wilkins said.

His sentiment was echoed by some of the other senior officers that had gathered at the front deck, one of which appeared to be Gruff-Voice, and whose name was actually Phillips.

"We won't know that until we find what lies within, will we?" she replied.

"What, if anything, could possibly survive within?" Phillips rasped.

Elisabeth gestured to it. "This thing has roamed or slumbered for hundreds of years, possibly more. There may be lost treasures, lost relics from other times. You all saw how it ate, it simply inhaled everything."

"But didn't the same breath melt all it touched?" Wilkins asked.

"Flesh, yes. But the Hog survived."

"Not unblemished, however."

She nodded. "True. There's still some risk to my plan, but anything that can survive such a duration within that worm is worth salvaging." Phillips opened his mouth to object once more, but she raised a hand. "Your opinions were invited as a courtesy, gentlemen – carry out my orders."

"Yes, Lady," the assembled men said before moving to their tasks.

Thomas approached. Even from their vantage point on the upper deck, the creature was still able to block much of the slowly sinking sun. "This cannot be a whim, surely."

"What do you mean?" she asked.

"You must know, or at least suspect, that there is something specific within that carcass."

"We'll find out soon enough."

A voice crackled over the speaking tube. "Take shelter now, for your own safety. I repeat, seek shelter now."

Elisabeth reached for the door, gripping the round handle with both hands and wrenching it open. "Let's watch from the pilot's control room, shall we?"

Inside waited a bank of heavy levers and dials, no doubt used for monitoring the many boilers, the whole thing resting below a narrow window of glass and steel mesh. The window ran the length of the dome. While the turret could rotate; there was a big periscope not far from a ladder, which in turn waited beside a closed door – perhaps access to the gunner's room above.

Several leather-backed chairs had been bolted before the levers, but Elisabeth didn't take any, instead she leant over the controls to stare out the window as the Hog began to back away from the corpse. He frowned. Did she arch her back just a little? As if to draw his eye? Or had he simply been staring at her anyway? *Idiot.*

He joined her without speaking.

Overhead, the heavy clank of the main canon being loaded was muffled, but when it fired, the vibrations rattled the handles in the control room.

The massive ball tore into the upper portion of the worm, striking at the centre of its significant length. The next shot hit lower again, and the third much closer to the ground. A fourth and final strike followed, tearing into a similar point of the beast's body.

All the while, the Hog was backing up until finally it stopped, then the dials on the main boiler began to rise as pressure built. Once again, the speaking tube echoed through the tank. "All hands brace for ramming manoeuvrers."

Thomas took one of the seats and Elisabeth followed, placing her boots against the steel of the control panel. He copied her action as the Sand-Hog started forward once more, quickly gaining speed.

"Will that window hold?" he asked.

Elisabeth nodded, even as she reached out to pull a lever. Blast shutters slid down over the window. The main canon fired again, and a countdown followed, the speaker crackling when it reached three.

Thomas gripped his knees and braced himself.

Impact rocked the Sand-Hog. His head nearly bounced from his knees, chest straining, but instead, the chair gave a mighty creak. He exhaled heavily. Below, the engines roared, and the pressure gauges rose further... and then the Hog was moving again, turning before coming to a far gentler halt.

"I told them the wedge would be enough," Elisabeth muttered as she pulled the lever for the shutters. They rose smoothly, smearing worm-flesh over the mesh but the desert was clearly visible, the sun falling quickly now.

"We don't have much light left," Elisabeth said. "You'll accompany me."

"I'd just as soon as return to my cell," he said.

"Too bad."

He glared at her but followed. There was little use fighting her over it. *She'll simply find something else to use as leverage.* And maybe an attempt to have her feel indebted to him was worthwhile? *If that's even possible.*

***

On the ground, men gathered with lanterns, aided by bigger searchlights from the Hog, beams that even now were being adjusted to fall upon the ruined carcass. The blightworm had been torn in half by the Hog, whose armour had dealt with the worm's corrosive innards well enough, and now its separate halves were slowly drooping as they dripped and decayed.

Once again Elisabeth had smothered any objections with her will, and now wore a diving suit of steel, one that matched Thomas' – difficult to move within, and difficult to see out of properly too, despite the generous window in the helmet. Doubtless, he would have personally found it easier to move within than Elisabeth, but she was no wilting flower. *I hate to admit this, but she's a little like Mia – they're both so strong.*

Elisabeth waved for him to follow and she started into the worm. A piece of flesh fell from above, striking her shoulder as she moved. Thomas joined her, waving an arm to get her attention and raising his voice as he did. "Even with this face-mask and helmet, I don't think we'll last a long time in there."

"If we find what I'm looking for, it won't take long – but you'll need to carry it." She resumed walking, heading for the left side.

"What is it?" His steps squelched as they started into the worm.

His breath fogged up the window in his helmet but not enough to stop him seeing. The inside of the blightworm was slick with moisture and black blood. Droplets and globs of flesh fell from the top of the carcass – several stories above – and which, for now at least, was holding in place. *If it falls, we're buried alive.*

His steel boots crunched over bones and shards of rock, pieces of steel, and things he couldn't identify. One piece might have been a horseshoe, others could have been swords, saddles and even guns.

Elisabeth waved him closer, pointing without words.

A large piece of steel was revealed, something like a corroded wheel-well or another part of a steam car.

The deeper they walked, the sharper the taste of copper became, even with their precautions. Her lantern had yet to reveal anything special either – not that he had any idea of what she was searching for.

"I think we need to—"

"There."

Elisabeth stepped closer to one of the walls. With each step, her boots stuck fast; she had to wrench each one free to reach her goal. His own boots were just as difficult to manage but he soon joined her where she crouched over something that glittered, growing brighter as she wiped away the gunk.

Her reinforced gloves hissed as she worked. His own suit creaked when he bent to help her. Within a few moments, he found himself growing short of breath and a drop of blood fell from his nose, striking the window. "What is it?" he asked.

"Something very valuable – it's called Orichalcum." She was smiling behind her helmet. "Bring it along. It will be very heavy."

He gripped the hunk, straining to even tilt it at first. The thing was only head-sized, but it was far denser than iron or lead. Thomas braced himself and lifted with his knees, exhaling as he stood. Another few drops of blood ran from his nose. Once he'd lifted it, moving was a little easier but his steps were still slow.

Elisabeth trailed him. "If only we could search the whole worm."

Thomas didn't bother answering.

Light from the Sand-Hog grew as they neared the cloven section and finally footing was easier. All he had to detour now were pools of the acidic blood, no more sucking innards. *Just a little further and I can get this damn thing onto a cart.*

"Thomas!" He'd barely taken two more steps when something crashed into his back. He fell forward, stumbling to his knees, Orichalcum rolling from his grip with a thud. Something crashed to the sand behind him, rotting flesh splashing across his back.

Thomas wrenched himself around.

Ooze covered a serious-looking hunk of stone; gunk continued to drip from the ceiling of flesh even as he took another step back. Elisabeth stood on the other side of the slab, her suit covered in the worm's decay. She wiped at the window on her helmet before pointing at the Orichalcum.

Thomas bent to retrieve it with another grunt. The slab of stone, which had obviously lodged in the worm's gut at one point, had been big enough to cave-in his helmet. He was lucky, damn lucky.

And confused.

Did she save me? *Or was she just worried about the Orichalcum?*

Chapter 15

Delilah fed and housed them again, this time without requiring manual labour.

She sent Javier to begin rounding up their supplies, while Christopher worked on what he'd need for the ship, leaving Ethan and Mia to plot a course through the ruins, which were unstable at best, considering their crumbling nature.

"Have you explored much of the city?" Mia asked Ethan from where she sat in the quiet parlour, wedging herself deeper into the plush chair. *This isn't too far removed from the palace.* Delilah had already retired, claiming some weariness but Mia had her suspicions. It seemed the woman was still convinced Mia and Ethan *needed* time alone.

And despite her fear, Mia couldn't deny that being alone with Ethan was hardly unpleasant.

"Only the edges, I'm afraid. I was never given the opportunity to travel much deeper," he replied.

"Was Williams pursuing you?"

"No." His voice grew quieter. "We were doing the pursuing – it was a long time ago; and a story for another time, perhaps."

"Of course." *Who was he pursuing exactly?* It didn't seem the right time to press him, though half a dozen questions still formed. Instead, she focused on the ruin. "What do we need to be wary of within the edges?"

"Not much, thankfully. Nature is slowly taking the place back; I remember whole buildings reclaimed by earth and grass and flowering vines, weeds growing between every stone. The steel has long since rusted and few buildings stand, there's not a single shard of glass left in any window. Toward the centre, I saw several towering structures, twice the size of the palace. One has fallen against another, or at least, they were still standing back then."

"And the centre?"

"We saw smoke; no doubt runaways are still there today. Best to avoid them."

Mia nodded. Few runaway camps welcomed strangers. *And why would they? The risk was always too great. So many had turned Thomas and I away the minute they saw the yellow tattoo.* Worse was being called a spy for Williams.

Ethan shifted, the creak of a chair joining the faint movement of his silhouette. "This map seems as good as any. I suppose we had better get some rest."

"Good idea," she said. "Sleep well."

"And you." He started across the room, his footfalls slowing as he neared the door. Mia held her breath a moment, waiting for the handle's squeak. Was he going to ask if she wanted help returning to her room? Something else?

Delilah's home seemed awfully empty all of a sudden.

Poor Javier was still out and Delilah herself had rooms at the other end of the building. *It's just me and Ethan now and we still haven't discussed or even acknowledged... whatever it is between us.*

Unease gripped her – did she even *want* him to mention it? If he did, it had to be confronted and now that the moment was seemingly upon her... *I don't know what I want to happen. Why? Why am I so confused?*

But the answer was obvious.

You're afraid.

Before she could speak, before she even knew if she was going to speak or what she'd say, the door opened and closed softly.

"Too slow, Mia," she said, and stood with a sigh.

She made her own way into the hallway then turned left, walking the thirty steps to her door. She reached for the handle, making a slight adjustment, and entered.

Within, the window let the faintest blush of moonlight into the room but she closed the curtain and sat on the bed, unlacing her boots. She lay back a moment, then fluffed her pillow before shifting her arms to get comfortable; they were lead pipes, surely, just like her legs.

Despite her weariness, Ethan wasn't the only thing on her mind.

Gatehouse refused to stay in the past. Since the first traces she and Thomas found in the north – the lever, the symbols and the photo album, the *Clara*, and the latest journal – it was clear the old rebellion would hold the key to her success now. *If we could just find a way to use the* Clara, *we could be free of Williams for good.*

If Golden Lakes bore fruit. If a pilot could truly be 'made', and if Thomas could be rescued from Elisabeth and, not in the least, if Williams could be held at bay. *A lot of ifs.*

Though if one thing worked in their favour, it was the fact that Williams didn't seem to know where she and Ethan were.

She blinked and yawned so wide that her jaw gave a tiny crack.

Fine, I'll go to sleep.

But sleep seemed brief – she was drawn quickly into another vision, a vast field of grey with green shooting stars streaking across a midnight sky. They spun, twirled and dove in swooping patterns as she watched, tiny pieces sometimes breaking off to explode into sparkling shapes that appeared to be letters or numbers, though none formed firmly.

Beyond the realm of the vision, dimly she was aware of what seemed to be a serious increase in visions lately, but what that might mean, if anything, was yet to be revealed.

A figure was walking across the leeched grasses now, head and shoulders touched with green light. It was a spindly thing with an oval head and a smooth face that lacked eyes – yet it bore a nose and mouth.

"Greetings," it said when it stopped, towering over her but making no threatening moves.

"Who are you?" she asked.

"Inconsequential."

"Very well. What do you want to tell me?"

"That your growing will attract the wrong attention before too long."

"Meaning?"

"Be wary here."

Ominous. "And where is here?"

"A place between dream and vision, between today and tomorrow. The chromata. You are well-versed by now."

"Am I? I don't feel that way."

"Inconsequential."

She frowned up at it. "Did you come to tell me anything else?"

"Yes. Remember the rat who wears a suit?"

"Yes." Her vision from the desert, right after she and Thomas escaped the Hog. How long ago that seemed now. "Is that who I should fear?"

"No. You will find him in the ruins and you will be a part of the time of his death."

She straightened now. "And who places this burden on me? You, strange man?"

"That too, is inconsequential," he said, and his mouth broke into a smile, though it faded quickly. "Remember, this place will not always be safe."

Mia reached for one of his hands, to stop him, but her fingers found naught but air. "Wait, how do I protect myself?"

The figure was nearly completely transparent now. "See what you want to see, and you will survive."

"And what if I don't want to dream like this?" she demanded.

"Inconsequential."

Mia put one hand on her hip. *Should have seen that one coming.*

Chapter 16

Thomas had not seen the supposedly wondrous Orichalcum since hauling it onto a handcart, a handcart which he then had to load into the Sand-Hog's lower levels, driving it up the wooden ramp by brute force more than grace or design.

And now he'd been afforded a wonderful luxury – a bath and a change of clothes. Coupled with that luxury was a rather dubious honour, however... another opportunity to dine with Elisabeth.

A command to do so, truly.

Even as he dressed anew in clean black clothing, including his very own flak jacket and boots, he found himself shaking his head. *It's still possible to run. You're not chained up; you could steal the steam car down below.* Or was he lying to himself? If he avoided all the guards, somehow brought the Hog to a halt, snuck the car out and then managed to outrun the monstrous tank, where was he running to?

Which direction would he gamble? They'd been heading roughly west since Last Castle for over seven days. Just how much water would he need to steal? Far more than he or a single car could carry.

You're a fool if you try and a fool if you stay.

Outside the private bathing quarters – whose, he had no idea – Thomas was escorted by a tired-looking guard to a certain point and then left to walk the final passage alone. *Just like before – only this time, will Fox appear?*

But Thomas reached Elisabeth's door without encountering the softly spoken snake. Even so, the man's orders stirred Thomas' own curiosity. Exactly what was Alita's Shell? Yet he had to navigate Elisabeth's motives, along with his doubt and confusion too – would he even be able to work the conversation around to such a topic?

Has she even invited me here for conversation?

Perhaps she meant to make her offer once more, the lie about freedom.

Thomas rapped on the door.

Elisabeth admitted him with a smile. "I trust you plan to stay this time? I hate to disappoint my cook. He has worked quite hard and it is the last of the chicken. After this it's lizard and desert fruits or some dubious salted meat."

Thomas moved to a seat right positioned of the head. "Is the Orichalcum living up to your hopes?" Before him were heaped various pieces of chicken, from wing to thigh and breast, pots of gravy and white sauce, steaming green vegetables and carrot too. Some of the foodstuffs he'd rarely seen while on the run and it was a true feast compared to what he'd been eating lately. His mouth watered. *Damn it.*

"A little early to say," she replied as she took her own seat at the head of the table and lifted a fork. "Eat, Thomas."

This is a mistake. But he loaded his plate with food then

poured gravy; his first bite of meat was so rich he actually sighed.

"Cook is a marvel," Elisabeth said. Once more, she watched him as she ate. "You might remember I asked you about your knowledge of our history."

"I do."

"And having seen the *Clara*, I assume you are at least aware of Gatehouse?"

Thomas gave a slow nod. "They were the owners of the airship."

"And more. A thorn in the side of the Williams dynasty for years, the only truly successful rebel force – at least, until they imploded. But after their demise, Williams' great grandfather set about locating and claiming all Gatehouse property."

"Like the *Clara*."

"Yes, but he could never figure out how to launch it – a special key was never found." She paused to take a long drink of wine. "But there are still ships and valuable technology that hasn't been reclaimed, strongholds yet to give up their secrets."

"Your detour?"

"Yes."

"And you need me to help you gain access? Some sort of steel door?"

"Naturally. After seeing what you did in order to enter the *Clara*'s hiding place... well, no-one else, short of Silas himself, could do that. I need you, Thomas. And I can offer you – and your sister – the freedom you so desire. There is something within Alita's Shell and you will unlock it for me."

Thomas lowered his fork. *There it was – the very words he'd been told to look for by Fox. And what of Silas? Did Elisabeth mean that he could work with steel the way Thomas did? Or that he'd use his potions? And if so, why hadn't Williams had The Alchemist do just that? Was Silas as much a prisoner as anyone else working for Williams?*

"You hesitate – I do not blame you for doubting me, Thomas."

"No. It's Silas, what did he do to me? You must know."

"I know little."

"Then tell me that much."

"Once you grant me access to—"

He leant closer. "This isn't a carrot you can dangle, Elisabeth. Prove to me your word is more than dust, tell me what you know and I might begin to believe you will offer me my freedom."

"There's that fire," she said with a chuckle, though rather than being dismissive, there seemed a touch of approval to the sound. "Very well. You were one of several children chosen to test Silas' potions when you were but a babe – no doubt over the objections of your parents. I know you were the only one to survive the tests, but I know nothing else."

Thomas stared at his plate; the room had receded, becoming tiny and dark all of a sudden. *Experimented on since I was a babe? She mentioned mother and father. Why couldn't they stop Silas?* He blinked. *Because they were slaves, idiot – that's the only thing that makes sense.*

A hand fell upon his shoulder and he flinched.

"No need for that," Elisabeth said, her voice soft, near his ear. Still he tensed, even as a pleasant tingle crossed his skin. Her curls fell across him as her lips brushed, so faint as to be ghostly, against his neck. "I've told you how wonderful our arrangement could be, Thomas."

He exhaled, pulse quickening as his entire body continued to react – like an ache. *By God, I'm supposed to hate her. I can't trust her. I should stop her. Stop this.* "You did."

"Then give in; I've seen you look at me, Thomas." Now one of her gloved hands tilted his cheek, their lips grazing. Her green eyes were bright with desire, fierce despite her gentleness now. "We can help each other."

She's manipulating you.

Thomas kissed her, pressing his lips against hers.

Elisabeth pulled back, but she was smiling. "I think we'll be more comfortable somewhere else."

He followed her around the table and to one of the adjoining doors – which led to a bed-chamber lit with candles. *She's planned every detail.* The thought was fleeting; Elisabeth gripped his jacket and drew him to the foot of the bed where she kissed him once more, her teeth gnashing against his, drawing blood.

"You'll free me of this place," he said, breathing hard.

"And you will unlock Alita's Shell."

She's using you, but you only need to use her too; that's how you survive.

Thomas gripped her shoulders and shoved her onto the bed, then flung his jacket aside.

Keep your enemies closer.

Elisabeth pulled him after; he leant over her, ripping her shirt as she tore at his. Her smooth skin was almost golden in the candlelight and Thomas let her draw him closer and then, finally, he let go of his doubts and rationalisations and stopped thinking altogether.

Chapter 17

Thomas woke to darkness, a warm body pressed against his back, an arm slung over his chest. *Elisabeth.* He could feel her breasts shift against his skin as she stirred, and her fingers began to slide down his stomach.

He caught her hand.

"Wait."

"That wasn't what you said last night, Thomas," she said, a hint of reproach in her voice. He flushed; at least she couldn't see his face.

I'm weak.

And he'd betrayed himself. Mia too. *She will be devastated.* Guilt was already worming its way into his stomach; how easy it had been to ignore all of that last night. To lie to himself. To pretend he was in control of what was happening. *Better make something of this, fool.* "This changes everything," he said.

"Meaning?"

"I mean, my standing here on the Sand-Hog. I'm not going to be treated as a slave; I'm your co-conspirator now.

Or were you planning to hide me in that cell? Call me to your room to sate your needs?"

She laughed. "No, I believe my men will accept your... promotion quite readily after that performance of yours with the blightworm."

"Good."

She pulled away and a chill replaced her warmth. "Find your clothes if you can and I'll explain what happens next."

Thomas rose, circling the bed for his clothing and concealed a wince at finding his shirt halfway across the room, torn at the front. Nearby, Elisabeth's own clothing had been rent nearly into tatters. *By God, am I a man or animal?*

Elisabeth now wore a heavy robe and was already waiting in an adjoining room, the light from a window casting everything in a pale blue. By the sounds, she was working on breakfast.

He joined her as he pulled on the jacket, which was in one piece at least, and she nodded to a pair of steaming cups. A rich scent filled the tiny room, big enough for a stove, bench and pantry only, the window lighting her hair as she spooned sugar into the cups.

Thomas gaped. "You have sugar... *and* coffee onboard?"

"It's not fresh but it's better than nothing," she said with a shrug.

He lifted the cup and inhaled. *Here's something I was never allowed to even go near in the palace.* "You think a slave would know the difference?"

Elisabeth frowned at him. "You don't have to drink it."

"I've never had the option to *refuse* coffee before, it almost makes up for years of being denied safety and happiness."

"Do you want to lecture me or win your freedom?"

"I think there's room for both."

She stepped closer, eyes hard. "Don't make the mistake of thinking you were the only one to suffer in that place."

A baseless claim, surely. And even if it was true, it never stayed her hand when it came to me. Or Mia. But he set the cup aside, untouched. "Fine. What do we have to do?"

"Remember what I said about Alita's Shell?"

"You need me to gain access."

"Yes." She took a sip of her coffee. "It's a site within the Federation. Before we reach it; we'll need to bribe the highway governor at Hameda."

No doubt the Sand-Hog has enough money for that task. "Where is Hameda?"

"A few days beyond the oasis. From there, we can strike out for the mountains and reach the Shell."

"And there's another giant door made by Gatehouse, like the cavern that holds the *Clara*? That's what you need me to tear through?"

"Yes and no. It's not simple to explain, in fact, it's far easier if you see it for yourself. But I don't believe Gatehouse made Alita's Shell at all, though they doubtless used it."

"What do you mean?"

"I've seen their symbols at certain points."

"And what do you believe lies within the Shell?"

"Freedom, Thomas. As I said before, the key to freedom."

"A functioning airship?"

She shook her head. "No, something greater."

"You're quite certain."

"Yes." She took another sip.

Thomas folded his arms. "How? How do you know the

Shell contains something that powerful? You've never been inside. This might all be a fool's errand."

"No, Thomas. There are volumes in Silas' library that suggest otherwise, and I trust them. Their words are burned into the backs of my eyes," she said, voice growing fierce.

Silas? Had Elisabeth been working with The Alchemist somehow? *Or had she simply stolen his knowledge?* And if Silas knew about Alita's Shell and the man had 'created' Thomas to tear through steel... Thomas reached for the coffee and took a long drink, the unexpected bitterness almost welcome. "You've stolen Silas' idea, haven't you?"

Now she sneered. "Stolen? How does one steal from a thief exactly? No, believe me, Thomas, no-one owns knowledge. It is free to be taken by all and any with wits enough to do so." Her expression softened, and she set her cup down before moving forward to press her body against his, running a hand along his cheek. "We'll reach the oasis soon. Time for you to prepare for more water harvesting."

And then she returned to the bedroom.

Thomas shook his head. Perhaps no-one owned knowledge, but it seemed Elisabeth still owned him, one way or another.

***

Thomas hauled another drum onto the cart, water sloshing over the side. It splashed onto his arms but it was welcome beneath the punishing, midday sun. Beside him, two men laboured to replicate his task.

"Wish I had your arms," one said with a grin. He was a

younger soldier with a wide smile.

"Shut-up, Peterson," the second man grunted. He headed back for the oasis, where lines of soldiers were working with their own barrels and tanks, the last few now, judging by Wilkins' orders. The oasis itself was more like a deep rock-pool, guarded by small ridges of stone and thin, scattered trees of green.

As the last few barrels were hauled from the water's edge, a figure strolled toward the water – Elisabeth. She was unarmed and wore no shoes, no coat but otherwise she was fully-clothed as she approached the water. At the edge, she seemed to give a sigh before stepping out and diving beyond the shallows.

"Get them onto the Hog," Phillips barked as he stomped by.

Thomas gripped the push bar of his trolley and strained, the smiling guard beside him. "Thanks," he said.

"Any time."

Together, they pushed the water over the uneven ground to the Hog and then up the ramp. By the time they entered the shadowy storage bay and off-loaded the water to waiting hands, sweat was pouring from Thomas' body. He found a steel crate and sat atop it, the faint tingling ever-present.

"Here." Peterson was holding out a canteen.

Thomas took it and drank before handing it back with a nod. "What's happening down there?" He jerked a thumb over his shoulder.

"Oh, The Lady? She does that each time we pass this way – once she's done we're allowed in. Really takes the edge off the job."

"I don't doubt it," Thomas said. *And I'm glad we harvested the water* before *scores of sweating, occasional bathers leap in after her.*

"You going to take a swim?"

Thomas shook his head. "Just some rest is enough."

"Right. See you later then."

Now that they were nearly done with the oasis, the next hurdle would be Hameda. Supposedly, an orderly place; most runaways either stayed to work or moved on and Williams' men were not always permitted to pursue, given how strained relationships had sometimes been between Kingdom and Federation.

Would Elisabeth have enough to bribe whoever needed to be bribed?

He hopped from the crate with a sigh; no way to know until they reached the town. Now, food was a bigger priority – if he was lucky, there'd be someone cooking in the mess hall. When he reached it, Thomas found half a dozen men grouped only loosely together, seemingly smaller for all the emptiness around them.

The sound of meat sizzling came through an open door.

Few glanced up as Thomas approached the kitchen, raising his voice a little. "Is it too early to get a meal?"

"Not a problem, just find a seat," came the reply.

Thomas chose an empty table and sat with his back to the soldiers. Maybe it would be enough to discourage conversation, maybe not. *Worth a try at least.*

He hadn't been waiting long when a soft voice spoke over the nearby murmur.

"Well, Thomas. Now that you've escaped the lion's den, we should find time to talk, don't you think?"

Fox. Thomas twisted in his chair.

None of the soldiers in the room were facing him; all seemed intent on their meal or low conversation.

He stood. "Who spoke?"

The nearest turned. "Something wrong, slave?" his voice was deep, entirely unlike Fox.

Thomas folded his arms. "Like Williams isn't your master, dog."

"What the hell did you say?" The man gripped his fork in white knuckles now.

One of his fellow diners placed a hand over the arm holding the fork. "Take it easy, Brenton." His voice was nothing like Fox's either.

Thomas glared at the other men, trying to commit each face to memory – one with a scar, one with white hair and a dark beard, another a little plump, mousy brown hair. The others, having a similar, grizzled look. Only one seemed young.

But none spoke another word, several returning to their meals.

"You want to talk, then you know where to find me," Thomas snapped, then started from the hall, appetite vanished. On his way, he glanced at a fellow who sat slightly alone. The soldier merely looked back with dull eyes. *Pricks. It could be any one of them.*

And obviously all or certainly most of them were working with Fox.

No shortage of trouble, then.

I hope Elisabeth has finished her leisurely dip.

Chapter 18

The breeze cooled Mia's face where she leant against the *Fleet*'s rail, the scent of salt strong on the water, waves breaking against the hull. The ocean was calm off the southern coast too, making for a pleasant journey so far – only a day from Tamas. *Pleasant except for the nights.* Cramped conditions and the threat of the chromata ensured poor sleep but at least she had not returned there yet.

"A few more days and we'll make landfall," Ethan said.

She nodded.

"Have you been pulled into the chromata again?"

"No," she said with a sigh. "I don't know if I dread or crave it, to be honest. I know I'd sleep better if I could just face this danger the guide mentioned. At least then I'd know what to expect."

His hand came to rest upon hers. "You will be its match, whatever it is."

She swallowed – at the touch, or was it her doubt over the chromata? "I hope you're right."

"I am." He removed his hand and the rustle of pages being

turned, followed. "I read this again last night and wanted to run something by you, see if you agree with me."

"A missing page?"

"No, just this part about the Gatehouse stronghold 'hiding more than our lives'."

"Remind me of the rest?"

"He writes: 'Part of me must thank God, or whoever watches over us, for the stronghold has yet to be found despite a brush with disaster in the skies over Brinhale just yesterday. I worry so, for it is hiding more than our lives; it is hiding a part of our future too.' I know we dismissed it as not being very useful before."

"Right. The air battle doesn't narrow down a location simply because it occurred over Brinhale."

"I agree. But what about the end there? What exactly did he mean by 'future'? The writer has mentioned something similar before. Maybe we've been focusing on the wrong part of the entry."

"It's too vague to know."

"Yes, but what's something obvious worth protecting that might ensure the future safety of Gatehouse?"

Mia snapped her fingers. "Knowledge."

"Exactly."

"And if we must 'make a pilot' then the best chance of doing so is if the stronghold has not been pillaged. And if we can find it."

"Can we assume it hasn't been discovered already?"

"Maybe not. The Williams line found the *Clara* – it's possible they already stole whatever specific plans or directions they needed from the stronghold, but the ruby heart is the only reason they failed to make her fly." She reached up to touch the key through her shirt.

"If so, I wonder if they ever tried to replicate the key."

"We're pinning a lot of hope on this stronghold," Mia said.

"I know. It might not contain any important knowledge at all; Gatehouse could have moved it during their war, the Williams' could have destroyed it. But we have to gamble."

"Golden Lakes will offer another clue, I know it."

***

"Gods watch over you both," Christopher called down.

Mia thanked him from where she clung to the longboat. "And you, Captain. Don't spend that loot all at once."

He laughed. "Worry not, some of it is hidden away somewhere for tomorrow."

The sailors beside her grunted as they worked the oars, droplets of water landing upon her. The swell was not precisely rough, but the rise and fall steady enough – she tensed as her stomach flipped. *This is new.* Was it not being able to judge the waves? Sailing aboard the *Albion* and to a lesser extent the *Fleet* was quite different, far more stable.

"Is something wrong?" Ethan asked.

"I'm sure it'll pass; it's the rocking."

The longboat soon hit sand and splashing followed as Ethan and the sailors leapt out. They dragged the boat up the beach, then Ethan helped her free. Her boots sunk into the wet sand a little, the cold tide splashing against her ankles.

"Good luck in there," one of the sailors said – Stephen.

"That storm will probably catch you before you cross the city."

"I think you're right," Ethan said, going on to describe dark clouds in the distance. "We'll find shelter in the outskirts, there're a few buildings that we can start with."

"Come and visit us one day," he said.

"We will."

They set out then, her feet sinking less and less with each step until she left the beach, where Mia found herself relying on her willow rifle more often with the uneven ground, half dirt or tufts of grass but while she did stumble, pack tugging at her balance, she rarely fell. Ethan would sometimes catch her arm and together they traversed the more broken ground. Clouds soon passed over the sun, but the storm did not immediately break, though a wind whipped up its share of dust.

"There's a stone wall ahead," Ethan called. "We'll stop there a moment, I want to use it to get my bearings."

"Right."

At the wall, Mia removed her pack and leant against the still-warm stone and exhaled a moment. It was good to be shielded, however temporarily and partially, from the wind. Ethan's boots scraped on the wall as he climbed. "What do you see?" Mia shouted up.

"There's a wide depression in the land ahead and beyond it I can see the edge of Aderlen. We've got at least four possibilities for better shelter than this, thankfully."

"Outposts?"

"Mostly intact. They're spread quite wide across my view, but we should reach the closest before the storm hits." He paused as thunder rumbled, still distant. "That's a little nudge, I guess. And there's lightning to go with it."

"I'm ready."

He thumped to the ground. "It looks like we're near an old road, it slopes down but it looks clearer."

"Let's try it."

Thunder pealed again, not so loud that the threat was immediate, but Mia did her best to quicken her pace. The abandoned road was somewhat smoother, but she quickly found that at the pace Ethan set, it was better to grip his hand.

"Sorry, I know I'm slowing us down," she said.

"No need to apologise," he replied. "We'll beat the storm."

Thunder followed them as they hurried on, and the wind now brought heavy drops of rain with it but when Ethan finally slowed, it hadn't grown much heavier. "Let's see what this one's like then. There's a hole in the roof and the window's empty."

"Can we shore up any of it?" Mia asked.

"I think so," he said. Once again, he took her hand and guided her. "You'll have to duck a little, the entryway sags."

She did so, and within, the hum of the wind died away but there was a gap somewhere that whistled. Her shoes crunched over debris and weeds as she moved away from the faint 'bright' shade that represented light from the hollow window.

"This is the only room that's good," Ethan said. "It's got four walls with three openings to deal with. We could probably use the tents for the door and window and then close off some of the roof for a chimney."

"I'll start on the window," Mia said.

"Right. I'll take the roof, then collect some firewood."

Mia set her rifle and pack against a corner wall, then

released the straps that bundled the heavy canvas of the tent. Then she found tent poles and the hammer, moving to the window. There, she drove the pegs into the mortar between stones before tying the canvas in place. As she worked, scraping sounds from Ethan echoed from above. The canvas snapped and bounced in the wind, but it seemed to be holding at least. *If it pops open in the middle of the night, we'll have a wonderful surprise.*

Ethan soon returned, the sound of wood clattering to the floor. "I'll get to the door in a moment, there's a slab of steel that I want to drag in place first."

"Need my help?"

"It's not too bad," he said. "I'm betting Thomas could manage it with one hand, but I'll still get the job done." It sounded as though he grinned as he spoke.

"You'll do fine," she said. "I'll start the fire."

When Ethan had blocked off the doorway and reinforced their efforts as best he could with whatever materials he'd been able to find, Mia offered a steaming cup of tea she'd boiled over the now steady fire, which hissed at the occasional drop of water from the makeshift chimney.

"Thank you."

Outside, the wind roared. Thunder continued to ring out across the land but as the room warmed, her sense of the storm began to recede. It was still out there, but both the blanket wrapped around her shoulders and the cup of tea in hand soothed her.

"How does the last of the beef sound?" Ethan asked.

"Perfect."

He rummaged around in his pack and the sizzle of the pan soon followed, the rich scent of meat filling the abandoned building.

"Do you think any of the stories about Aderlen are true?"

"That it was destroyed by a vengeful God? Or that it was once shifted five hundred kilometres by giants?"

She laughed. "Actually, I meant the stories of the city beneath the city. Did you ever see anything to suggest that it's true?"

Fresh sizzling rose as he flipped the meat. "No, but it's not as far-fetched as the giants. Are you thinking of the rat?"

"It does seem an obvious place for a rat to hide."

"Maybe you'll get another vision tonight?"

She nodded.

"If you want, I can stay awake tonight to watch over you," he said. "Wake you if you seem in danger."

"That wouldn't be fair – you need to rest too."

"You only have to tell me if you wish it."

"I will," Mia said. "But I hope it won't be necessary."

"Let's eat first anyway," he said, putting some lightness into his voice for her benefit, it seemed. "Who knows? Maybe my cooking will be so wonderful you'll fall into a deep, dreamless sleep of satisfaction?"

She smiled. "I hate to break your heart, Ethan..."

He laughed over the sizzle of the pan.

Chapter 19

But she did dream.

This time, the chromata deposited her on a towering mountain peak, snow gleaming as if afire where it lay beneath a gargantuan moon; the bone-white orb covered nearly a third of the entire horizon. It was so unnatural that she simply stared at first, only gradually becoming aware of the sound of scraping on stone.

Smaller sounds, like clawed feet.

She peered over the edge, toward the vista of moonlit forest below, pine needles swaying in a seemingly absent wind – at least, she couldn't feel it from her position. But she could see a rat in a suit, struggling to climb up to her. And even as she crouched, she knew that if she helped the rat to the top, it would somehow die. If she did nothing, it would plummet to its death.

What choice is this?

"No choice, of course. It is a punishment." The voice bore a hollow sound, as if struggling up from the depths of the grave.

Mia spun.

A tall figure stood a mere half-dozen paces away, the cold stare of a bull's skull resting in place of a human head. The bone was weathered but the horns were black and sharp, gleaming in the moonlight. A long red cloak covered the figure; dust stirred from the shoulders, rising in tiny puffs to swirl down and stain the snow, despite the lack of wind.

"Who are you?"

"Nyath, protector of chromata."

Mia folded her arms. "You're no protector."

"Your very presence defiles this place." Nyath stepped forward and as if between a blink, appeared directly before her.

She stumbled back.

A hand of flesh and bone shot forth, catching her by the throat.

He squeezed.

Mia clawed at his grip, but it was iron. Black began to seep from its hollow eyes, staining the skull an uneven grey. Her surroundings dimmed, and it was more than the air being denied her – and it shouldn't have mattered! *He shouldn't be able to do this, I'm dreaming, aren't I?*

Yet the warning from the guide had been clear enough. What else had he said?

Something about seeing... her memory failed, as though her very mind was collapsing. No! Mia kicked at the robe as she hung, aiming for a kneecap, but her feet found only air.

She dug her nails into his flesh, but the bull's skull revealed no pain and more blackness poured forth, streaming down the bone to drip onto her face. A chill spread, something so cold it seemed to touch her very core and when spots splashed onto her hands Mia thrashed harder – her flesh had disappeared, revealing the bone beneath.

Snow exploded around her.

Mia hit the ground. She rolled, gasping for air as the dark film cleared from her vision, from her mind. She rose to her knees, bracing herself.

The spindly guide stood between her and Nyath, its frame taller than before. It reached out and splayed its elongated fingers; they formed a web-like barrier that seemed as much a symbol as an actual impediment.

"Begone," the guide commanded.

Nyath hurled himself forward, only to be driven back by the guide's power. "This is forbidden."

"Inconsequential."

"You cannot protect her every time." And then Nyath flickered and disappeared.

Mia slumped onto her haunches, breathing hard. She lifted her arm – the flesh was whole. Yet her throat was tender when she swallowed.

The guide shrunk a little as it turned, still towering over her as the eyeless head faced down. "You must return now – but please be better prepared tomorrow night."

"Then I'll return here? You know that?"

"Yes. Remember what you were told, you must see what you want to see if you are to survive the chromata."

"But what does that mean?"

The guide was fading already. "That your will must be stronger than your opponent. See what you wish to come to pass."

Mia leapt to her feet. "You're saying the same thing!"

Her voice echoed across the mountains but her only

response was a swift darkness which, just as suddenly, became a new, warm darkness that was accompanied by the sound of bubbling water and crackling flames.

The ruin she and Ethan had transformed into camp.

I'm safe.

Mia shuddered, as if to shake off the final traces of Nyath's touch. She reached up to touch her throat... still tender. A chill ran over her body. *This is far too real.*

"Mia?" Ethan's voice.

She rose to a sitting position, her limbs aching as she did. *As if I've been sprinting, this is terrible.* Her blanket was not upset, had she tensed her body the whole time, yet not thrashed about?

"Were you pulled into the chromata again?" he asked.

"Yes." She swallowed – it was uncomfortable to talk. "And he was there, the one I was warned about."

"Are you hurt?" he asked.

"A little. He was throttling me in the dream but I feel it now."

Ethan moved closer and his tone hardened; a mixture of anger and worry. "Your throat is bruised. We need to do something."

"I know."

He sighed. "I don't know what to suggest."

"How about some of that tea, for a start?" she said.

"Good idea."

Ethan prepared the drink then gave her the cup, sipping from his own as he waited. His finger tapping on the tin cup seemed like hammer blows compared to the crackle of the fire; his frustration poured from him.

"The guide told me I'd dream again."

"Before, he said you had to 'see what you want to see and you will survive', is that right?"

Wish I'd been able to remember that when Nyath had me – did the darkness weaken my mind? "Yes, those were his words. But I don't know what they mean. I wanted to escape but I couldn't."

"It sounds deceptively simple... yet strange, considering your vision."

"Perhaps. In my visions, I see things almost as they are, I believe, as if my sight were restored. Only everything seems exaggerated, which still doesn't help with the guide's advice."

"Well, what about the one who attacked you? Is there anything to learn there?"

"I don't know." She described Nyath, focusing on the appearance and the strange blackness. "He called himself Nyath."

"Unusual name."

"Yes. What does it mean?"

"I'm not sure... it reminds me of my childhood. There was something similar, something mother used to tell me and my brothers. A fairy tale? A legend? A demon that haunted dreams? Only, I don't remember the skull."

"Let's keep thinking while we break camp."

"Right. We can work on a plan for the night too – I'll stay awake this time."

"I'm not sure that you'll know... I don't think I moved or even cried out."

"I'll know," he said, firmly.

Mia hesitated, despite the rush of comfort his words brought. *He might not be able to wake me at all – do I really want to put him through that?* The sense of Nyath's hands on her throat returned like an unwelcome echo, but no more than a ghost.

Maybe I don't have a choice. For now. *If I could just figure out what the guide meant. It has to be so simple that I'm overlooking it.*

Ethan's hand came to rest on her own. "I will protect you however I'm able – and even if it ends up being true that I cannot help in your dreams, let me be your shield by day."

She smiled. "You already are."

Yet doubt lingered; not over his words but for the coming nightfall. It already seemed so close, mere hours away. She repressed a shudder. *How can I defeat something like Nyath?*

Chapter 20

Their boots clapped on stone and her willow-rifle clinked along ahead of her. Much of Aderlen's streets were cracked or broken, plagued by clumps of grass. Rain from the storm had left behind the beautiful scent of petrichor, of water on earth and stone and she breathed deeply. Pleasing as it was, however, it did not banish the lingering threat of Nyath.

He was a faint presence on her mind as they travelled; lurking beneath the focus she had to spend on navigating the ruin. Several times her rifle found large holes or twisted heaps of rubble, Ethan warned her about the larger ones, but he had to watch their surroundings as much as their path – yet so far, there'd been no hint of anyone else in the ruin.

Admittedly, they were still on the fringes only. "How far have we come?" she asked at noon, pausing to drink from her flask. It eased a headache that she'd only half-acknowledged to herself – was it due to stress, dehydration or eye-strain?

"Perhaps a third of the way into the southern end. Remember the towers I mentioned? They're further west, still standing. It looks like one has slumped even further but it's still there. Vines are still climbing from the base and I can see black shapes flying around them. The clouds are lingering."

"I didn't realise Aderlen had so much rain."

"There's enough to keep things fairly green around here, true. The Sunken River helps, though I suspect it poisons as much as it feeds, the deeper you travel."

"Will we encounter it?"

"That probably depends on the rat. Have you felt anything new?"

Only the same fears about Nyath. "Nothing yet."

"Then we'll keep on for now. There's a reasonably intact structure ahead that might be a good place to stop. I know I could use some food."

She nodded, though nothing in her pack truly appealed and not because their supplies were lacking. *It's that bloody Nyath.* Was he watching now? Was that possible? She didn't even know if he was spirit or flesh, let alone *why* he wanted to stop her entering chromata. *And what did he mean when he mentioned a punishment?*

When they reached the building, Ethan described a wide, ruined room with uneven walls, frames empty of glass. White tiles were crumbling, long-since stained and what little copper remained for taps were blue with patina. *A bathhouse.*

"At least these stone benches are still in one piece," he said.

Mia used her rifle to find the nearest and sat, searching her pack for an apple, yet she did not bite into it, instead she held the fruit and listened. Something lurked beneath the crunching from Ethan and his own apple. A regular thudding rhythm, muffled...

"Can you hear that?" she asked.

The crunching stopped. "No. What is it?"

"It's like footsteps." She stood. They seemed deep, as though a faint vibration accompanied them. "But I think they're *below* us."

"I hear it." The click and clack of Ethan's twin-shot followed his words. The rumbling grew louder too. "Whatever's happening, I don't know if we've got time to avoid it. Keep your rifle ready."

"I don't feel danger." But she still gripped the weapon, resting a fingertip against the trigger.

Steel screeched, followed by a clang.

She swung her weapon toward the sound but did not fire. *There's no threat but what's happening down there?*

"Don't shoot us," a voice called. It echoed, as if from a tunnel. "We'd like to talk."

"Who are you?" Ethan asked.

"Representatives from Brightnest."

"Which is?"

"May we exit?" a new voice asked. "It'll be a lot easier to explain if we're not clinging to this ladder down here."

Ethan stepped closer to Mia. "I want to see your hands when you do."

"Our weapons are holstered," the first voice; younger, replied.

"Good."

Grunts of effort seemed to bounce off the tiled walls and after a moment, the older man spoke once more. "My name is Anthony, and this is my little brother Francis. We've been sent as guides."

"By who and to where?" Mia asked.

"Ah, to Brightnest, ma'am," Anthony replied.

"The Boss sent us," Francis added. "He knew you were coming and we confirmed it earlier; we're on sentry duty today."

"You have sentries here?" Ethan asked.

Mia missed the man's answer. *How did this so-called 'Boss' know that? Is he like me? Or is there a simpler explanation? Could it be Nyath?* She couldn't prevent a frown. *Highly unlikely – that was her fear talking, right? Stupid. No, these men seem honest and my Gift is silent, we can probably trust them at least for now.*

"... we're able to travel quite far using them. There's a few places where we have to head above ground again but we'll be there by evening if you're willing to accept the invitation."

"We'd like to know a little more about your leader and camp, first," Ethan said.

Francis replied. "Well, the camp's pretty organised now. It's been growing for a few years now – maybe nine already, right Anthony?"

"Next winter, I think."

"Right. So we call it Brightnest and there's about fifty of us runaways there – we celebrated our fourth birth just last month."

"What of Williams?" Mia asked.

The sound of spitting preceded Anthony's words. "He hasn't sent anyone here for at least three years now. At first, we'd see hunting parties but they must have given up. We don't have a lot of firepower, but we've been able to scavenge some impressive stuff from Aderlen."

"And there's Michelson too," Francis added.

"This 'Boss' you keep mentioning?" Mia asked.

"Nah, Michelson is a merchant. He swings by once a season," the younger man replied. "Boss was the first. He's the one who brought us all together. Before him, there were a few tiny camps here and there, but things are better now."

"You said he knew we were coming?"

"Right. Sometimes, he just knows things before they happen – it's amazing. The new Runners never believe at first but it don't take long."

Then he is like me.

"And what did he say about us?" Ethan asked.

"That two important ex-slaves were going to pass on the outskirts and that any one on sentry duty had to deliver his invitation. Boss says he has information that can help you." A pause. "What was that name again, Anthony? That old group of rebels."

"Gatehouse."

"Yeah, Gatehouse. Boss said you'd know who he meant."

"We do," Ethan said, and Mia sensed him turn toward her. "Maybe we'd better pay your leader a visit, then."

"Agreed," Mia said.

Chapter 21

Elisabeth leant against the rail at the prow, the tiny deck crowded by Thomas, Sergeant Wilkins, and two men guarding the door, sweat trickling from their temples as they faced the afternoon sun. Both fellows Elisabeth claimed she trusted implicitly, as she did Wilkins.

Thomas had no choice but to trust her judgement in turn.

It seemed she still considered the recent report on the ongoing repairs, some of which were on hold while the Hog travelled once more. The beast of a machine still ploughed through sandy earth and by the frequency of detours or thumps, it would soon be time to raise the plough and rely only on the treads.

"Are you concerned?" Wilkins asked her.

"They will be done when they are done, and that is fine. No, I find myself wondering about the burials," Elisabeth said. "Is it enough to have left them in Federation land?"

"We had little choice, truly," the sergeant said.

"So we decided," she said before looking to Thomas. "Very well, tell me what all this is about and hurry it along."

He glanced from face to face. "You have snakes aboard the Sand-Hog."

"Then he's finally made contact; this is good," Wilkins said with a nod.

"What?"

Elisabeth motioned to the two guards and they stepped back into the hallway, doubtless taking up positions there. "We know about Fox and his cubs," Elisabeth said. "We were hoping you'd draw him out. So, what has he been asking of you?"

Was she ever going to mention him to me? Thomas explained his meetings in brief. "He is especially keen to learn about Alita's Shell and he's expecting to speak with me soon."

Elisabeth smiled. "Then let's give him something juicy to chew on." She addressed Wilkins. "And then we'll need to look at that passage again, Sergeant. And I want another count; see how many are ours in case we need to move soon."

"Of course, my lady."

"You're not confident in your men?" Thomas asked. *Just how many blasted snakes are on this tank?*

"I'd stake my life on two-thirds of the Hog being loyal to Lady Elisabeth before Williams," the sergeant said.

"You're doing exactly that, aren't you?" Thomas asked. "And now mine, too. Which two-thirds? How many snakes are you sure of?"

"Be calm," Elisabeth said, her voice growing firm. "We have everything in hand. The best thing you can do is feed whatever misinformation that I give you to Fox."

"Only if he buys it."

"You'll make him buy it – and he'll want it, because it's going to be *exactly* what he craves."

"Which is?"

"That he'll get his chance to strike once we open the Shell. It's what he and Williams are waiting for – ever-since I made it clear to the old timer that I am not returning the Hog, that she is mine now."

Thomas held up a hand. "Wait, when did that happen?"

"Don't worry about when."

"I think I should."

"When I realised that I knew better than he. Move on, Thomas."

She wasn't going to budge – but that didn't mean he wouldn't keep trying to find out. "Fine. So Williams is expecting you to lead him to the Shell? Does he think that you're not aware of his plant?"

"Yes. He's a daft old fool, too obsessed with his mechanical toys. He is over-confident, and assumes I am heading for the Shell and that I believe I have gotten away with my so-called theft."

"Are you sure?"

She shrugged. "He's obviously waiting either way and he cannot reach me from Brinhale in any event."

"Isn't that what Fox is for?" Thomas asked.

She raised an eyebrow. "I appreciate the concern, Thomas, but everything is well in hand."

Wilkins cleared his throat. "I believe I will start on those tasks before we reach Hameda, my lady."

"Please," she said.

"Come and see me in the armoury again, Thomas," he said as he left. "I'd appreciate your help."

"I will."

Once the door closed, Thomas turned back to Elisabeth,

who was watching the sandy plains roll by. The land was still mostly desert here, not dissimilar to Williams' Kingdom. *How meaningless the lines on maps are to the earth – it shouldn't surprise me.* "What lies will I feed him?"

"That is something I will whisper to you tonight," Elisabeth said.

Thomas tried to repress a shiver of excitement at the thought of returning to her bed – or maybe it was a shudder of disgust, disgust with himself. As much as he craved the feel of her skin against his own, as much as he told himself he had to play at being her slave in order to escape, he knew it was barely an act at all. He was caught and he was, each night, betraying Mia. Betraying their past. *You're a damn fool, Thomas.* "And what do I say to him in the meantime?"

"Everything you've learnt from me so far."

He hesitated. "Truly?"

"It won't be anything Williams wouldn't have already shared. Fox is testing you – just make sure your answers line-up with what he already knows."

"I see." He glanced ahead; the haze of smoke had appeared before the Hog's path. "And what of Hameda?"

"You will find it an unremarkable place. Welcoming to Kingdom slaves, fairly industrious. Though they do produce an interesting drink, you might enjoy it."

"I meant this highway governor."

"Bareo. It is his job to ensure the roads between Hameda and other towns are safe. He is a cheerful fellow but quite ruthless beneath it," she said. "You'll meet him when we make our delivery in any event. But now, why don't you return to my rooms and bathe. I'll have a meal prepared for us."

Thomas shook his head. *Now I'm being sent to her room? I ought to shove her over the rail.* Instead, he started for the door, opening it and muttering to himself as he strode along the dim corridor. *You* want *to wait for her – and that's the real problem, isn't it?*

At the opposite end of the corridor, the walkway widened to make room for men to load one of the lesser canons, a single lamp burning and one man on watch; he was sleeping on his feet, slumped against the wall beside the cold boilers. *I should wake him; spare the poor sap Elisabeth's wrath... unless it's one of Fox's men.*

But a fierce tingling spread through Thomas' limbs – rushing over him as if his anger at himself had cloaked its approach. Or was feeding it? Yet the sensation did not ease. *This isn't another moment of adjustment like every other time.* Thomas slowed at a hint of movement. Had one of the high stacks of cannon balls shifted ever-so slightly? Steel screeched on steel.

Is it moving?

The highest crate shot down toward him.

Thomas dove forward.

A mighty clang rocked the passage and then he tumbled to a halt against one of the walls. He found his knees, one arm raised but no other missiles flew from the stack and the tingling had eased.

The crate lay shattered and even now, cannon balls were rolling from the wreckage. The guard was blinking, hand on his weapon, breathing hard. "What's going on here?" He took a few steps forward, a deep frown coming across his face.

Thomas kept his gaze on the remaining crates. "A fine question, soldier."

Chapter 22

Highway Governor Bareo sat behind an enormous steel desk, a large map spread before him, tiny markers arranged along the dark lines. He was indeed a cheerful man and he became yet more cheerful when Thomas rested a sack of star-dust on the map.

"Splendid, this is a far brighter day now," Bareo said, his rolling accent slight. He gave the bag a pat then began to hum as he swiped the drugs away and dumped them into a creaking drawer. "You do indeed find yourself very welcome on our highways, Lady Elisabeth." He produced quill and paper next, writing out a short missive and then affixing a crimson seal to the bottom before handing it over.

"It's a pleasure to visit the Federation once more," she said.

"No doubt, especially compared to that drab world you usually inhabit." He winked at Thomas. "Don't you agree?"

"Very much." Even if the dusty streets of Hameda hadn't appeared cleaner for the most part, even if the buildings didn't bear pleasing coloured tiles on their rooves, and even if the few peach and melon gardens they'd passed hadn't seemed so plentiful, he would have answered the same.

Because one difference made all the difference.

No slaves.

Like a livelier version of Silver Rock, the generally more-tanned Federation folk, many wearing dreadlocks like Carlos, were joined by their fair share of runaways and ex-slaves, in what appeared to be a rather harmonious existence. Hameda's militia seemed relaxed too, leaning on their rifles, even as they kept a watchful eye on the desert or their citizens.

"No need to rub it in, Bareo," Elisabeth said.

He raised his hands in mock acquiescence.

"So, what can you tell us of the road east?"

"Heading to the Shimmering Ranges again, I see."

She nodded. "Worth another look."

"Well, there has been talk of brigands lurking to the north. A little more organised perhaps, but nothing that would trouble your Hog, I suspect."

"Good."

"Actually..."

Elisabeth shook her head. "That's not part of our arrangement."

"I wonder." His hands formed a steeple before him. "What if the people of Hameda were to offer a little more than mere access to its beautiful roads?"

"We won't be using the roads themselves anyway, remember? Wouldn't want my tread to mulch them up."

"Haha, wait until you hear my offer," he said as he stood and crossed the room, stretching to remove a stitched volume from a single shelf. It bore no writing on the cover and a thin blue ribbon marked a page which he opened but did not share. "It is no secret that several… important one-time subjects of the Williams Kingdom sometimes reside within the Federation."

"True," Elisabeth said, wary curiosity in her voice.

"What if I were to divulge the false name and location of a certain individual that I am sure Williams himself would love to speak to once more?"

"What if I didn't believe you?"

He grinned. "Marianne Edwards."

Elisabeth leant forward. "No lies, Governor."

"You can indeed trust me on this. I know where she will be residing in a mere matter of weeks."

Thomas glanced between the two. It was clear Elisabeth was suddenly far more interested. But who was Marianne Edwards? *The name seems vaguely familiar… someone from the palace then? Someone David mentioned long ago?*

Elisabeth pointed at the man. "How does the governor of a place like Hameda know something like that?"

"I admit this is a quiet town compared to the capital, but knowledge is the lifeblood of my business – it is my job to know such things."

"Try harder."

Bareo raised an eyebrow, lips twitching as though he would smile.

"Who is Marianne Edwards?" Thomas asked, pouncing upon a chance to speak.

"Take a moment and you may remember," Elisabeth said, shortly. To their host she said, "Now, *if* this is true and you can provide information on Edwards then I will gladly exterminate whatever outlaws are troubling this place – but I will need far more than your insufferable insinuations."

Now he did smile. "Very well. You shall have it, but I will need some time to arrange such a thing. I will send someone out to that steel beast of yours tonight, I'm sure you'll find them very convincing."

She stood. "I hope they are." She waved a hand at Thomas to follow, which he did with narrowed eyes. Behind him, it seemed Bareo gave a sigh of satisfaction but Elisabeth did not turn and Thomas had more questions for her in any event.

***

Once again, he dined with Elisabeth, the distant rumble of the boiler and engines muted, though she seemed barely interested in anything he brought up – not the impending visit with Fox and the future misinformation she expected him to deliver – still withheld – nor the strange attack by the canons.

"It was probably meant to scare you, to keep you off-balance. Expect a visit from Fox soon," she said.

"They went to quite a bit of effort if it really was someone hidden behind the walls like you claim."

"Do you have another explanation?"

"No."

"Then move on, Thomas. It's like I said – Fox trying to unnerve you, and succeeding, I must add."

He shook his head. "Easy for you to say – it's not your life on the line."

She drank and set her empty glass down, hard enough that it rang. "My life is always on the line. And so has yours been, for all of your days, Thomas. You should be used to it by now."

"Don't ignore this just because you're blind to everything else now that this Marianne Edwards has popped up."

"Is your memory truly so flawed? Marianne Edwards is the queen, Thomas."

He frowned. *Queen Williams? Maybe Marianne was her name, but it was hard to remember.* No-one had spoken of the queen – it was long-since forbidden. "I thought she was..."

"Dead? Yes, her famous suicide from the walls of Brinhale is a fiction, though Williams' quest to stamp out any mention of her name in the palace is real enough. Once, when we were young, I asked Julian about his mother and the king overheard." She pointed to a thin white scar on her cheekbone, something he'd only noticed since he'd started sleeping with her. "That was my reward – knowing my vanity, he'd promised to draw his razor across my entire face but Julian stopped him. Earned himself a thrashing for it too."

Thomas couldn't find any sympathy for Julian but Elisabeth's earlier claim of being a prisoner there, of suffering herself, suddenly rang a *little* truer. Even so... *Is this story just another way to manipulate me?*

"You seem surprised, Thomas," she said, obviously having picked up something from his expression.

"I think it's best that we left the past right where it is now."

She raised an eyebrow. "You mean Julian? I've heard about how things... ended for him and I am not surprised."

Thomas gave her a look. "You and he seemed rather close."

She shrugged. "Didn't you want to leave the past alone?"

"I do," he said. "Except for the queen – what does it mean

if she's alive? If she didn't kill herself, what is happening?"

She rose and moved closer, threading herself between Thomas and the table to straddle him. "Now *those* are far more interesting questions. What indeed does it mean? For one, it means I have something else I can hold over that old fool. For another, we cannot let Fox learn of this because it is exactly the sort of thing he has been seeking for years."

Thomas glanced around at the walls. "Then you're sure of your rooms? Fox was using that passage outside before."

"I've long-since taken the necessary precautions, Thomas."

"Then why did the queen leave?"

"Why else? She desired her freedom, as do we all. Williams is more the tyrant than you believe, both with those around him and the very nation itself. You and Mia took up with that handsome rebel, Ethan Cameron, right?"

He did not answer. *I hope you're both safe.*

"No need to deny it, Thomas. My point is, you probably think the way Ethan does, you think of the king in terms of his military and technological might, yes? The soldiers in the major cities, the puppet governments and the larger forces along the border garrisons – enough to launch a considerable assault on the Inland Federation if he one day seeks their resources."

Williams' words on the palace walls echoed. *By the end of the summer, we will have enough to finally put down the Inland Federation once and for all.* "He fears other nations just as much."

She shrugged. "Maybe that's justifiable, maybe not. But what I'm trying to say is that he loves to control those closest to him, to possess them, but it is the minds of his citizens as much as anything else that he controls, that has made him so dangerous." She raised a hand. "And I don't mean that in any mystical sense. I mean, he has convinced so many otherwise good citizens that slavery is acceptable. That is his true power, his true crime."

Thomas nodded slowly. She had the truth of it, though such noble sentiment seemed odd coming from her. "The queen defied him?"

"Never openly, at first." Elisabeth removed a glove and ran her fingertips along his jaw. "I remember stories that suggested she did so in a very public way once, speaking out against him during a ceremony at the arena. And she was popular, Thomas, she might have one day started change."

"She obviously failed – how did she escape?"

"For that, you have to thank Silas or your friend David – and one other, above either of them."

"Who?"

"I believe you've met this person, Thomas. A former Bruiser; his name is Aiden."

A sharp rapping came from the door, interrupting Thomas' shock.

"Yes?" Elisabeth called.

"Lady, there is a woman from Hameda to see you."

"Bring her in."

Chapter 23

A young woman with flaxen hair, dressed in a belted tunic and leather pants entered the room. She was accompanied by a familiar soldier – the cheerful Peterson – who excused himself at a look from Elisabeth. Their visitor appeared at ease, though her gun belt was empty and she carried a single piece of folded paper.

"Lady Elisabeth and companion, my name is Felicity and I am here to allay your concerns over the highway governor's claims."

"Very kind of you, please sit," Elisabeth said as she stood, disentangling herself from Thomas smoothly.

"You're concerned that claims about Marianne Edwards are untrue, but I promise you that she can, at times, be found within the Inland Federation and, in a matter of weeks, will be once more."

"And what lends credence to your words?"

She lifted her forearm. A yellow hourglass sat on her wrist. It bore one significant difference from Thomas' own mark – a rose at its centre. "As a child, I was one of her scullery maids."

"If that tattoo is real, why do you betray her now?" Elisabeth asked.

"There is no betrayal. I am here only to say that Bareo's information is trustworthy – you do not have it, do you? In fact, all you have at present is confirmation of what has long been suspected in the east."

Thomas grinned. "She's got a point."

"Yes, she does. Very well, Felicity, tell me this. What does the queen have to gain by confirming such information now? Has she been waiting for someone from Williams' inner circle to drop by the Federation border towns, hoping for what? Information?"

"Her Majesty does not inform me of such things, of course."

"I suppose not," Elisabeth said with a smile. "I will have my men accompany you back to the town. You have been quite helpful."

"I hope so." She nodded to them both as she started for the door, which Peterson opened.

"Oliver, take Felicity and make sure she reaches town safely – don't let her out of your sight, Bareo mentioned bandits."

"You can count on us, my lady," he said with a smile.

Once the door closed, Elisabeth slumped into her chair with a sigh. She stretched her legs across the edge of the table, nudging her plate aside.

"Something is afoot, isn't it?" Thomas asked. "It's far too convenient that one of the queen's servants just happened to be in Hameda. Marianne must be close by."

"Or she has watchers in various locations, waiting."

Thomas nodded. "For what?"

"I hope to find out – let's see what Oliver and Sven bring back."

"They're going to follow her?"

She snorted. "I'm no fool, Thomas."

"I never thought you were," he said.

"Well, I think that's not the only spot of fishing I'd like to do tonight. Why don't you visit Wilkins in the armoury? He's been waiting for you anyway."

"You want Fox to 'visit' me, don't you?"

"Remember, Thomas. Be convincing but don't take all night – I still need one more thing from you."

He shook his head but started for the door. *Am I destined to be a slave always? To her? To my own blasted body?* But again, he did not argue but instead clenched his jaw as he stalked the passages of the Hog, heading deeper toward the armoury.

The old justifications were all there – leaping from his mind in an attempt to smother his doubts, his loathing. Using Elisabeth was the most likely path to achieve his freedom. At her side, he gained access to her plans, her knowledge and her weapons. Staying out of the cell made it easier to stay strong. And clean was a bonus.

With Elisabeth, he also learnt more about the threats that lay aboard the Hog.

And once again, he now had a very real chance of learning more about Gatehouse, which was the best chance to restore the *Clara*. Then he could find Mia and they'd finally escape for good. Whatever Elisabeth thought she'd find within the Shimmering Ranges she could keep, so long as Thomas got his own chance.

And isn't that all only half true? You still like sleeping with her far too much — and there's still a chance she'll try and kill you once you've broken in.

Thomas turned a sharp corner and thumped into a pair of soldiers, who gripped his arms. Someone kicked his legs out from under him and then they were holding him down. He swore, struggling enough to hopefully make it seem believable, but once a familiar voice spoke from behind, Thomas stopped. *Why bother?*

"Coming up for air, are we?"

"Ask your questions, already, Fox." He twisted his head but saw only the rivets on the wall and the knee of a man who held him.

"Eager to return I see. And why not?" he mused. "So, let's begin with the Shell."

"It is said to hold some great relic or technology from the past. It lies somewhere in the Shimmering Ranges," Thomas began. He continued to share all the details Elisabeth had offered, answering questions as they were posed. "Elisabeth needs me to open the way."

"Hmmm." Fox took a few steps closer, sounding pleased at least. "And what of the Orichalcum, it's purpose? Does it aid in entry?"

"I have no idea."

A new pressure came to rest upon the small of his back — a foot. "Truly?"

"Yes," Thomas grunted.

"I see. Consider that another request from your king, then."

Thomas waited through another moment of silence.

"And the young woman who visited?"

"Someone from Bareo," he said. Had his answer been too quick? Fox had him in a pattern of answering but such a vague response wasn't going to be enough – added pressure on his back caused him to gasp.

"Let's be a little more forthcoming, shall we?"

"She had an hourglass," he managed. "Yellow."

The pressure eased. "Isn't that fascinating? Go on, Thomas – what did she want?"

"Something about the roads, access to the Shimmering Ranges. Elisabeth has agreed to deal with some outlaws as part of the cost."

And now the man lifted his foot all the way. "Less fascinating. So be it. Thomas, I believe it is time to make your task a little more exhilarating. You are aware of a soldier named Oliver Peterson, I assume?"

"Why?"

"Because I will ensure he suffers quite the accident with the main boiler if you do not have the purpose of the Orichalcum for me by tomorrow evening."

"You think I care about him? About any of you?" He fed all the derision he could muster into his words, but Fox only laughed.

"Yes, I do. That's your most obvious weakness, Thomas. You care enough that I am quite certain you will have the required information for me." His footfalls began to recede. "Let's meet here again, shall we?"

Thomas grunted as the men released him and followed their master. He rose to one knee, looking after them but could not recognise any by the backs of their heads. It could have been any soldier from the mess hall or none.

No way to know.

And more, Fox himself had already disappeared beyond the limit of the lantern light.

"Bastard."

Chapter 24

The tunnels beneath the ruins were full of echoes: their boots, their voices, the trickle of water, the occasional bird cry from above that filtered down. The underground almost seemed more alive than the ruins. It was warmer, if nothing else. Safety was an issue, too. Whenever they left the aqueducts to detour blockage or other obstacles, the brothers had warned of mighty drops.

Mia walked tethered to Ethan, who in turn followed their guides on their trek toward Brightnest.

"Could you tell me more of your boss's gift?" Mia asked. "Has he ever described it?" A tiny bit of doubt lingered, irrational but persistent, about the man. Francis and Anthony hardly seemed like the type to idolise a creature like Nyath of course. And once again, her Gift offered no warning. *But what if Nyath can block that?* She swallowed, as if his hands had brushed against her throat.

"Says it's feelings, mostly. Or things he just knows," Francis said.

"What about visions or dreams?"

"Hmmm... he's never said nothing like that to me."

"Anthony?"

His footfalls stopped, and a wrenching sound followed, iron on iron. "Not to me either. He doesn't claim to fully understand it, but he trusts it and I trust him." He chuckled. "Like we said, it's hard to believe at first but you'll see soon enough."

Mia slowed as Ethan did and it seemed they passed through an opening – circular by the feel beneath her hands. *Still doesn't sound like Nyath. Good.*

"We're eager to meet him and learn his news," Ethan said.

"End of this passage and you'll get your chance."

Already, Mia could hear the faint hum from a large group of people – the passage of feet, voices, tiny clinking of tools too, and it did not take long for that to become loud enough for her to judge Brightnest to be only a few dozen feet away.

Francis soon hailed someone ahead. "Ho, the watch."

"That you and Anthony, Francis?" a woman replied.

"Sure is."

"Find those wanderers then?"

"We did. You can meet them," he said. "This is Ethan and Mia."

"Welcome to Brightnest," she replied. "I'm just as keen for whatever news you bring as everyone else here, but Boss wants to see you right away."

"I hope Ethan can do this justice," Anthony said as once again, steel hinges squeaked.

Ethan gave a low whistle. "Well."

The faint sense of strong light hit her eyes; her blindfold muted the impact but the sense of an expansive space was clear. The chatter grew too, and there was even a squeal of laughter from a child, the echo of a smith's hammer from some distance away almost lost.

"Mia, I don't think I can do this justice and I wish I could," he said. "Brightnest is a truly fitting name – it's underground, a town of stone and steel, mostly single-storey buildings. The magical thing is that it's illuminated by sunlight falling through to hit mirrors of all shapes. They've been placed all over, in the surrounding walls, on tall posts and even on rooves – streams of light criss-cross overhead, it's like a maze of pure light. There's a big, central mirror that smaller streams feed into, too. It's flat so it bounces up like a blooming bushel of light."

"You've done a fine job," she said. "It sounds beautiful."

"Agreed," Francis said.

***

According to Ethan, Boss's stone home was modest – large rooms but little in the way of luxuries. The upholstered chairs they now waited in and the crackling fireplace had been the most impressive items he'd noted as Francis led them within, Anthony having already left to check on his family.

Now they waited but not for long it seemed – brisk footfalls soon announced someone's approach.

"Here they are, Boss. Right where you said they'd pass."

"Commendable work, as always, Francis. Please, give your brother my thanks." The boss had a smooth voice with a cultured inflection – former nobility?

"I will," Francis said, sounding pleased. "Hope to see you

both again," he added as he left.

"Mia, Ethan, thank you for accepting my invitation. My name is actually Patrick, despite what everyone else seems to think, and I have the honour of caring for this fragile hamlet." He cleared his throat. "I find myself craving something to drink – can I bring you anything? I have a little whiskey left."

"Thank you, but I am fine," Mia said. Answers were probably more preferable.

"Please," Ethan replied.

"Just a moment." The sound of clinking glass filled the room. "I understand your curiosity must be rather pressing and I will share all that I know of Gatehouse, but I would ask for your patience a little longer. I have a boon to ask."

"You're afraid," Mia said. The sense of his fear was suddenly strong – it crossed the room between them like an arrow. *He's seen his death.* Patrick feared for Brightnest, for when he was gone. "You worry about your people."

"I do, greatly." But the man chuckled. "And how strong, your Gift. Just as David said – you are hope for us all."

She stood. "Who are you?"

"Mia? What's wrong?" Ethan asked.

"Please," Patrick said. "I am exactly who I say I am – Patrick Huntington, one-time nobleman from Williams' court of parasites. I am descended of the family who once ruled Aderlen but now rule only echoes. During my time in the palace Silas recognised whatever sliver of humanity I had left, and my slight ability for Farsight and thus I was recruited by Silas to help with a great undertaking – the end of the Williams Kingdom."

Huntington. The name *was* familiar; hadn't she heard

it around the palace, as a child? Back then, there'd been so many soldiers, servants and lords and more than a few royal bastards too, all expecting the same thing – instant obedience. The price of failure was always pain. After a time, the names blended into a single mumbled 'my lord' which was safer than making a mistake. "You know Silas? And David? What did he do to me and Thomas? And what of—"

"Mia, I cannot answer all your questions at once – nor will I until you hear my request, one which I hope you will take seriously."

She exhaled. "What do you need from us?"

"I need you to use your Gift to help me choose a successor here. I know my time is swiftly approaching. I know neither of us can prevent it, but I must do all I can to ensure the survival, the freedom of those who reside here. Fate has drawn you close enough that I was able to sense you; I cannot spurn such good fortune."

"And I cannot promise I will have any more luck than you," she said, unable to keep a touch of relief from her voice. "But I will try."

"That is enough, thank you. Now, I will arrange for the evening meal and then I will tell you all I can recall, all I have seen with my paltry ability. Please excuse me for but a moment."

"Of course."

"So, do we trust him?" Ethan asked, once Patrick had left. "You remember him from the palace?"

"I do. At least, I remember hearing his name a few times; I *think* he served in a few of the border disputes with the Federation. Maybe we spoke once... it was a long time ago. But I don't feel a threat."

"That's good enough for me," Ethan said. "What about his death? Did you see it too?"

"No. Nyath interrupted," she said, lips tightening. "But I know I'll be involved and I cannot stop it."

Ethan's hand closed over her own. "Maybe you can make a difference still."

"Or maybe I'll put us both in danger."

"Mia, I won't let that happen." A fierce sense of determination exuded from him.

She smiled, and surely her face must have revealed the sadness within. His was a beautiful thought but fruitless. "Ethan, you cannot make that promise, but thank you."

"Where I cannot protect you, you will protect yourself. You are so much stronger than you seem to believe."

"Perhaps." *But I am hardly a match for Nyath – and I can't avoid sleep forever.*

Chapter 25

Patrick served humble food, but it was filling, even if Mia didn't truly taste much of it. The threat of Nyath's next appearance lingered, but it was Patrick's words that kept her – and Ethan – mostly silent during the meal.

"I was not privy to all that Silas arranged, you must understand. David was my leader in the rebellion, a deferred-only rebellion as it now must seem. It was he who helped me escape the palace once we had been discovered."

"When was this?"

"Around the time you and Thomas were sent to the cells, I believe."

"You were imprisoned?" Ethan asked.

Mia nodded. "Beneath the Execution Tree – Williams sent us there, but David freed us. We could never figure out why the king tried to have us executed, and David didn't know either. And it never made sense, especially after all the efforts Williams later undertook to recapture us."

"Like his desire to have you produce more gifted offspring?"

"Yes. Or Julian's plans for Thomas to act as pilot for the Colossus."

A sharp intake of breath from Patrick followed her words. "That thing is still being developed? I had hoped it would fail."

"For my own part in the rebellion," Ethan said, "I managed to set its construction back but it will still be built."

"Thank you nonetheless," Patrick replied. "In any event, I believe David did know why Williams had planned to send you to the tree. It was a ruse."

Mia straightened. "What do you mean? Are you saying that David—"

"No. I meant our king. You and your brother were due to manifest your Gifts and he wanted you out of sight, like the rest of his most prized slaves – those who bear the Red Hourglass – those like Silas himself."

Even Silas? Perhaps it should be no surprise. "Silas too? We had suspected... but still, the ruse was needlessly elaborate for a king."

"Never underestimate the cruelty of man, Mia."

"True enough."

"And while I know not the full details, I know Silas works for his own freedom as much as that of the people in these lands," Patrick said. "But now, you must still seek Gatehouse?"

"We do."

"To aid in the resurrection of the *Clara*, yes?"

"Yes."

"Then seek as you have been, Golden Lakes for the markings of Gatehouse are to be found there." The sound of something being slid across the dining table was soft.

"Within that slim volume, you will find plans for the *Clara*. It is difficult to decipher, for me with no Gift for mechanical things but is vital nonetheless. I have held it since David entrusted it to my care."

"This is amazing," Ethan said.

"Patrick, we are in your debt," Mia added. With the plans there was a chance at last to make the *Clara* fly.

"No, you have already pledged your aid in my own task, that is thanks enough. And before you grow too joyful, you are aware that the *Clara* requires three items that have been scattered with other conspirators."

"You mean the ruby heart?"

"That is one, yes, but I sense you carry it already."

"I do." She frowned. "Wait, are you saying that Aiden was part of the rebellion?"

"Again, I don't know all the details but yes. It seems he had his own agenda, of course. The *Albion*?"

"Yes. He has taken it."

"That is regrettable – he wasn't an entirely bad fellow."

Mia held back her disagreement.

"You mentioned a third item?" Ethan asked.

"For safety, no single member knew more than where any two items were hidden, or who, if anyone, was nominated as keeper. I was only aware of Aiden; we rarely crossed paths, seeing as Williams' had him quite deep in the Federation much of the time. Aiden may have known where the plans were or perhaps he did not know of me and held the secret of the third key."

"And Golden Lakes will help us with that?"

"I hope it would be true, yes. David loved the places where Gatehouse had been, he said he left a copy of an important map there. I thought it a risk, but he countered that it was a bigger risk to have such knowledge held by one man only. Whether it is safe, or where it leads I cannot ascertain but I think it cannot be ignored."

"We must travel there," Mia said. "I was already sure of that much."

"Good," he said. "If you wish, I will accompany you there as guide."

Mia hesitated. "You said you have seen your death…"

"So it may be. But better I face it there, for if not, it will surely find me here."

"What is it?" Ethan asked, then cleared his throat. "Forgive my callous question, but I wish to prepare as best I may."

"The specific details are hidden from me," Patrick said. "All I know is that my time on this earth comes to a close either after Mia leaves or after I leave with Mia."

"I see." Ethan sounded troubled.

"I should add that while I did not see your own deaths, such a fact does not preclude suffering, but we will be assisted by two of Brightnest's finest. In truth, more wished to accompany us but that will not be necessary."

"Then you don't expect we'll be attacked by Williams or bandits? Rival camps?"

"There are no such camps, we have consolidated here," Patrick explained. "But I doubt Williams has anyone hunting, soldiers haven't been seen in far too long. More, I'd hoped a smaller group might be a harder target."

"And my judgement on your successor?"

"The two I deem most fitting will accompany us – I feel either would make a fine leader, but I cannot see far enough into the future. I pray that you will." Chair legs scraped on stone. "And now I must seek my rest. I bid you do the same; rooms have been prepared for you nearby."

"Thank you for all you have done," Ethan said.

"Of course."

The former-noble left and Ethan offered to guide her to their rooms. "Please."

At the door, Mia paused with her hand against the steel. Sleep waited – which meant the chromata and Nyath. *Should I ask Ethan to stay? If I'm caught, he probably won't realise it. And even if he does, will he be able to wake me?*

"Mia?"

"It's nothing; I just hope I can make the right choice."

"You will," he said softly. A moment of silence and then he spoke again. "My offer stands, you know."

She shook her head. "I have to face him sooner or later."

"And what of the advice you were given?"

"We know the guide said: 'See what you want to see and you will survive' and I have to believe it. Remember how I said that in the chromata I can see, my blindness is gone?"

"Yes."

"It's a vivid place. I think he's trying to say that I can shape it, that if I can imagine a thing it will be so. I have to believe that is what the guide meant."

"I've no doubt from what you've described, that anything is possible there."

"I'll know soon enough." She pushed on the door, her other hand reaching for the handle.

Ethan caught her shoulder. "Let me watch over you this night."

She hesitated a moment longer, then nodded.

Chapter 26

Slumber was slow to come despite the weariness bearing down on her – yet when it came, the chromata followed, smothering the vague sense of her bed and room, of Ethan sitting at the desk reading by candlelight.

In its place, a field of burning clouds.

When she walked amongst them, her feet stirred the fluffy white beneath wispy threads of golden fire that curled up. They bore no heat, nor crackling sounds. It was beautiful, and she paused to simply stare, enjoying the moment.

Yet after a time, the emptiness became apparent.

The place was still lovely, but the vast blue sky stretching above and the pale fire below – what did it mean? She started in one direction at a jog. With no sun and no landmarks, no land itself, she could have been heading in any direction, toward anything or nothing.

Ahead, something fell from the sky, punching through the clouds.

She slowed as she approached the hole.

A dizzying drop – the red dust of the earth far, far below,

the mountains like tiny bumps. She stepped back at a thin whistling sound.

A second shape was plummeting from above. It struck the clouds and a puff of white was left behind. Then another object hit, and a fourth. She gaped at the sky; they were silvery cauldrons, and they continued to fall even as she skipped back, giving them more room as they tore at the clouds. *What do they have to do with anything?*

She frowned up at one of the cauldrons hurtling down from the sky and traced its path. *Move.* It didn't alter course and she glared at it, grinding her teeth. *Move!* The shining object jerked to the side, clanging against another and she gasped.

"Hiding up here, are you?"

Mia spun.

Nyath stood before her, arms folded, skull-head impassive.

"Why do you stand in my way?" she demanded, clenching her hands to keep them from shaking.

"Because you do not belong here. This is my place." He flashed closer, faster than a blink, and rammed his hands into her chest.

Mia was flung back. She hit the clouds' pliable surface, rolling and clutching at them but it was not enough – she slipped through one of the holes with a cry.

Wind roared. It filled her ears and her mouth, tearing at her eyes as the red earth rushed toward her. Her limbs flailed as she tumbled over and over, heart crashing against the inside of her chest. *Do something!* The ground was flashing between red and blue and white of the sky.

She squeezed her eyes shut.

Land.

Land.

Land!

Her body slowed, and she screamed it this time. "Land!"

And then she stopped.

Mia opened her eyes – red plains stretched before her, dust swirling.

Distant mountain peaks stretched up to the sky but otherwise it was a featureless plain. There was no wind, no sound but the blood surging through her veins, her slowly calming heartbeat.

I'm alive. It worked... how did I do that?

Nyath appeared before her and advanced. "How tragic, your miniscule progress comes to an end so soon."

She backed away, trying to buy time. "Who are you?"

"Protector of chromata."

He leapt after her, once again moving too fast for her eye to track, and then his hands were squeezing her throat closed. She tore at his grip once more, even as her vision began to dim from the blackness seeping from his eye-sockets.

The cauldron!

She rallied her remaining strength, trying to break his hold with the force of her will alone, with her mind this time. And for a moment, just a moment, the pressure eased.

Then Nyath's shadow intensified.

At the same time a hot pain grew in her leg.

The chromata wavered, Nyath fading, the red desert and blue sky too – replaced by darkness. The heat seared, causing her leg to flinch and she woke, gasping for air.

Count your blessings, Mia.

Nyath's voice echoed in her mind.

And then it was replaced by Ethan's voice, he was calling

her name. "Mia? Can you hear me? Mia?"

"I do."

An exhale followed. "Thank the Gods. I didn't know if it was working."

"You were able to wake me?"

"Yes. You were rigid but twitching. You didn't make a sound – I might not have known if I'd been sleeping."

Pain still pulsed in her leg and she frowned, reaching for it, fingertips flinching away from a burn about the size of her palm. It was deep enough that she'd need to treat it but if it saved her life, it was worth the pain and discomfort.

"I used a candle," Ethan said, his tone apologetic. "I couldn't think of anything else, you didn't respond to your name or to being shaken either. I even slapped you once, I'm sorry."

She reached for him and his hand found hers. "There's no need to apologise, you saved me." And for the moment, that was enough.

***

Dawn was near, so she didn't bother trying to sleep again, instead preparing supplies and tending to her wound before she and Ethan met Patrick and two of the Brightnest members he'd chosen – one being Francis and the other, a woman named Selena.

"Have either of you travelled to Golden Lakes before?" she asked, her voice welcoming.

"Neither of us," Mia replied.

"Well, it's not a difficult journey but we'll do our best to keep you both from harm's way."

"There's an old bridge nearer the lake but that's probably the worst of it," Francis added.

"Then let us reach it swiftly," Patrick said.

Once they'd left Brightnest, the path became rougher, though nothing Mia couldn't manage at first. But as the day wore on the trail grew more troublesome – overgrown, snagging undergrowth and stones or even, at times, animal skulls according to Ethan.

When the day cooled to evening they'd reached a suitable place to camp, which Ethan quickly arranged while Mia worked on the elements for a stew, using a pot Francis had set over the fire. "Anthony and I took this from Brinhale when we escaped, sometimes I can't believe it survived all the time we spent before finding the nest."

During the meal, Mia fought the dread that had been growing – night would close in soon. Just how many hours could she stay awake? Ethan would rouse her if he thought she was in danger again but how long could she expect *him* to avoid sleep? Nyath wouldn't tolerate her returning. Would there even be any warning this time? She'd almost found a way to change the chromata. *I have to face him sooner or later.*

"How do you feel, Patrick?" Selena asked at one point.

"Quite weary but well enough," he replied, and Mia wondered if he were actually older than he sounded. "I feel no danger nearby, sense no trouble here or at the Lake. We'll reach it by noon tomorrow; the sun will break through the clouds and shine upon the ruined restaurant."

"It sounds somehow beautiful," Francis said.

"It is. As you know, I have visited the site several times. The water is dark but beautiful, sprinkled with leaves as it is

– but it is the sense of history that I, like David, was always drawn to. There is still a long bar and beneath it you can find empty bottles of wine from decades past and fragments of glassware fashioned in a long-disused style."

"And traces of Gatehouse too?" Ethan asked.

"You'll see their markings on some of the furniture and within a hidden storeroom, where not only the map lies, but even a few artefacts that survived."

"And it is all still safe?" he asked.

"It was some months ago."

"We've seen no sign of large parties of men moving there either," Selena said.

A good sign at least. But her heart was not in the thought and when everyone sought their rest, she volunteered to take the first watch, pacing a tiny stretch beyond the firelight, her mind a mess of doubt, fear, and discarded plans.

"You know, you should be listening," a voice said, some time later.

Ethan.

"I know. I cannot be still."

"I will watch over you again," he said. "I have my flame ready." He'd brightened his voice.

She nodded.

"Go, try and rest. I will be right beside you."

A tear formed behind her blindfold and she started back toward the faint sense of the campfire, finding her bedroll and lying down. She clenched her hands to fists as she waited for sleep – and somehow, despite her tension, the day's exertion drew her into slumber as it had each night.

Or maybe the chromata drew her in each night?

But once again, she faced more, stretching red plains

beneath a bright sun.

Try something before he finds you.

Mia went down on one knee and scooped a handful of red sand, then rose to toss it into the air. It drifted as it fell, and she stared after it. *Move.* The shape of the sand rippled, as though a sudden breeze had struck it.

She threw another handful into the air and pushed harder, feeding her fear and frustration into her effort. The grains scattered as if caught in a silent explosion.

Hands encircled her neck, lifting her from her feet.

Nyath!

Mia caught his hands but did not struggle – instead, she pictured his mask in her mind, and imagined bone covering over the holes. A grunt came from behind and the shadow pushed back, striking hard enough that she cried out.

"Your efforts are futile," Nyath hissed.

I'm not strong enough!

Panic set her to thrashing but a new voice roared. Mia fell, striking the sand with a thump. She rolled onto one elbow.

A middle-aged man with greying hair, quite thin and dressed in a dark suit of a fine weave, battled Nyath. He swung a polished cane, face a mask of concentration. His swings were not unlike that of a swordsman. Each blow was caught or deflected by Nyath's own arms.

"Flee, Mia!" the man cried – and it was Patrick.

Nyath spun, flinging his arms out and driving the nobleman back. He pivoted and struck Nyath a glancing blow across the horns.

"I can help you!" she shouted but he could not reply. Nyath was attacking faster and faster, his arms blurring until the cane snapped. The next blow tore into Patrick's chest and he collapsed, striking the earth without a sound.

Mia cried out.

This is my fault!

Nyath advanced upon her, one hand dripping blood.

Something flashed across the red sand, flitting around Nyath to leap at her – the small, brown and grey shape landed on her hand. A rat! Its body was bent and bloodied but the jaws still snapped over a finger.

The shock broke the chromata's spell and she woke to darkness, Nyath's voice ringing in her mind. *And so your final card has been played.*

"Mia?" Ethan, beside her once more – he spoke instantly, as if he'd been watching her.

"Where's Patrick?" she asked. "Someone, check on him, quickly."

"Boss?" Francis asked. No reply. "I need light."

Scrambling sounds and then the fire seemed to bloom and nearby, someone, possibly Selena, worked on a lantern.

But I know what they'll find.

Patrick had sacrificed himself. Did he lie? Did he know how it would end? And still he walked toward it without fear? No-one deserved such an end. *He's stronger than I'd have been.*

"He's gone," Francis said.

Chapter 27

Mia stood beside a stone cairn as someone whispered a prayer beneath the sun. The faint breeze carried the scent of green, of plants and water, the trickle of a stream this time, instead of the hot wind of the desert when she'd said goodbye to David, so long ago now.

Her duty to Patrick weighed upon her mind. Her debt also – and more, the fear that came with another night, though it was still hours away. *How will I survive it? If only there was a way to spend more time there without Nyath interfering.*

"We'll take you to Golden Lakes and then return to Brightnest," Francis said, his voice heavy with grief. "A bigger party will come and retrieve the boss."

"You can leave now, if you wish," Ethan asked. "We can find the way."

"No, it is no trouble," Selena replied.

"Thank you," Ethan said. "If you are ready, we should try and get a march on the sun."

"Of course."

Their path followed that of the stream until noon when

the trail rose, and Mia found her calves straining, but when they hit even ground once again late in the afternoon, it was with a sigh of relief and the sense of accomplishment that she paused, hands on her hips.

"There's the Span of Leaves," Selena announced.

"Not a bridge of leaves, I trust?" Mia asked.

"No. We're fine now, but the cedars and willows can bury the bridge in leaves and make a slippery surface. Even the hand rail can be unreliable."

"And beyond?" Ethan asked.

"See the hill on the other side? Golden Lakes is in a little depression."

"We'll see you there and then start back, if you don't mind," Francis said. "I want to make sure The Boss is safe."

"You've done much for us, already," Mia said.

Ethan guided her to the bridge and she kept one hand on the rail as they walked, occasional squeaks following but it was a sturdy construction, no swaying and wide enough for three abreast, it seemed. Below there was only quiet, which seemed odd for a bridge.

"I don't hear much in the way of flowing water," she said at what Ethan told her was the halfway point – twenty-six steps.

"The river was once much, much bigger," Francis said.

She strained and was able to make out faint trickling sounds from below, but it quickly faded, then returned. As though several small streams now passed beneath the span.

"That's the last of the bridge," Ethan soon said, as the rail ceased beneath her grip and underfoot, softer walking. Shade followed as they passed beneath rows of trees, which Ethan described as tall and green, then they were standing atop the crest, Golden Lakes below.

"It's just like in your vision," Ethan said. "Only long since abandoned. The lake is quite broad and still. Nearby the winery's roof is starting to collapse at one end, the stone is covered in moss but the glasshouse or dining hall looks a little more solid."

"No glass but plenty of rusted steel," Francis added.

"What of the decking?" Mia asked.

"Just a few stumps in the water now – must have been a real pretty place long ago," he said.

"No signs of movement. It's probably still abandoned but we can search it with you if you like?" Selena said.

"There's no danger," Mia said softly. *But David's map is here, I feel that much.* "Thank you for staying with us. I hope your path home is not filled with pain only."

"It will be difficult," Francis admitted.

"I hope we can meet again soon," Mia said. "I would like to pay my respects at his final resting place... and there is something else."

"A decision he wants you to make," he said.

"Yes. I fear I have not yet been able."

"Please don't rush," he said. "Neither I nor Selena are in any hurry."

"Truly?"

"Of course," Francis said and Selena added her agreement and then the two started out.

"Ready?" Ethan asked.

"Let's see what awaits us."

Mia used her rifle to guide herself across the earth but once she found flagstones, she slung the weapon over her shoulder and joined Ethan in passing between the wide, empty opening. Gravel and ancient glass crunched beneath their boots as they crossed the dining floor. According to Ethan there were only a few rotting remnants of tables but the bar at the back, where the greenhouse adjoined the main building, was still mostly intact. "There's a chunk missing from one end and the surface is covered in droppings and leaves, but it's here."

She leant against the bar a moment while he rummaged around.

"Similar labels but no intact bottles here – I assume the rest of the building will be the same," he said.

"Thirsty, are you?" she smiled, and the feel of her cheeks changing was almost odd – had it been so long since she'd smiled?

"Just checking for hidden switches or levers," he said with a chuckle.

It was cooler in the main building, the unpleasant, musty scent of rotting wood stronger. The room seemed large, perhaps a spacious hallway or reception area, but also to hold little of interest since Ethan led her to one of three doors he found – giving it a thump to pass, warped wood had probably changed shape over the years.

"Anything?" she asked.

"The kitchen, I think."

"What about upstairs?"

"Give me a minute."

They returned to the main room and Mia waited until he called from the opposite end. "The stair is ruined; we might need to scale the outside."

She nodded. "Must be the third door." Saying it aloud seemed right.

"It leads down – probably the cellar."

"Maybe you'll find your wine down there," she said.

"Only if the looters have been fantastically lax over the last few score years."

"Or if Gatehouse is better at hiding things than you're giving credit."

"True, my lady." More rummaging sounds followed and then the rasp of a match as he lit their lantern. "Ready?"

"I am."

"Use me as a guide if you like."

She rested her hand on Ethan's shoulder and together they stepped down into darkness, a damp scent growing, intensifying as they reached the cellar floor.

"Rows of wine racks here, all empty or smashed so far. Too bad cobwebs and dust aren't as valuable."

"Can we circle the room? I think the obvious thing we want is a hidden room."

"Right."

They moved in the hush, Ethan pausing at times to describe what he saw or to deal with webs. As she followed, the sense of their target became clear... both above and below... but not the upper storey of the building.

"We've almost come back to the stair," Ethan said.

"It's above us," she said, certain now. "On the ceiling, there's something there."

"Could you raise the lantern?" he asked. She held out her hand and found the handle. "I think I'll need my rifle for this."

"Do you see something?"

"There's marking on one of the boards of the ceiling, almost as if..." a click followed, then stone ground against stone, right beside her. Cold air flowed up from beyond.

"Another set of steps?"

"Yes," he said as he retrieved the lantern. "Time to find that map."

Once more, Mia used Ethan's shoulder and they descended, soon coming to a long passage that carried more cold air and dampness. "We're beneath the lake," Mia said. *Maybe that explains the wavy nature of my vision about this place – what we need is technically under water.*

"Hopefully Gatehouse and David were as obsessive about their waterproofing methods as their secrets."

"David would have taken every precaution," she said. He'd always made her check locked doors twice, made her be sure about where she wanted to move.

The passage ended at a steel door, which Ethan forced open. "Surprised it wasn't locked."

"If there's a strongbox it will be, no doubt," Mia said. She reached up to grip the ruby heart where it still hung around her neck. "What do you see?"

"It's a small room with a huge strongbox – just as you said," he replied. "Nothing else."

"Is it locked?"

"Yes." His next words came from nearer the ground; he'd obviously knelt. "And the lock looks familiar."

She lifted the key from around her neck. "Like this?"

"Try it," he said.

Mia knelt beside him, feeling for the lock – the box was bulky steel, bigger than a keg, like a modest kitchen table even. She fitted the key within and turned.

A solid click.

Yes!

She gripped the handle and moved back, swinging the door wide.

"It's here," Ethan said, excitement growing in his voice. Then he laughed. "And a bottle of wine with a note attached. 'For whoever finds this, use the map in good conscience and let a glass be raised in a toast over the ashes of the Dirt Kings.' It's signed David."

"Oh." Mia swallowed. Like a message from beyond the grave. "What of the map?"

"It's actually engraved on a sheet of steel... it looks like it leads to... The Mist of Dawn."

"From the journal."

"Right." There was little excitement in his voice. "But the names don't make sense, the Thunder Forest? I know of no such place on the continent; it sounds like a fairy tale."

"And that's where this Mist of Dawn lies?"

"Supposedly."

"Can you read the other places to me?"

Ethan did so, reeling off a handful of names that bore little to no familiarity. One was *Victona*, which was vaguely like Viterra but nothing else seemed of use. "Is Victona a city?"

"The map only marks circles, not images," Ethan replied. "It could be a town or a mountain, no way to know. Perhaps the map is older than it seems, older even than Gatehouse."

"We need to copy it anyway," she said. "Then we can plan our next step."

"Which should probably be to set up camp," he replied. "Perhaps the kitchen, it's good shelter and should be easy to heat if the night turns cold."

The night.

A chill fell across her. "Good idea," she said, her words flat.

Somehow, she'd forgotten Nyath, forgotten that she'd have to sleep, have to return to the chromata. It had been the thrill of the chase, the promise of progress. *And now I'm out of chances; I can feel it and Ethan cannot stay awake forever. Nyath will find me and kill me.*

The certainty of her impending death carried its own bloated dread, weighing upon her shoulders, pressing upon her chest. Somehow worse, was not knowing where the certainty came from.

Is it my fear or my Gift?

Chapter 28

Once again, the Hog thundered along largely empty lands – a little greener than much of the east perhaps. For now, they ran parallel to an impressively well-maintained road of stone. So soon after dawn, the highway appeared quiet but Thomas wasn't given much chance to focus on it from his position on Elisabeth's private balcony, as the Hog pulled away to detour a stand of trees – after which, it continued north.

Ahead, dark trees lined a box canyon of yellow stone. It was quite large – a single narrow path leading within – and as they drew closer, signs of fortification. Low stone walls surrounded rifle positions or a sentry post concealed between the trees.

"They've certainly got a lot of warning," Thomas said.

"Little good it will do them," Elisabeth replied.

He folded his arms. "Do we need to do this? Is information about the queen truly worth more than whatever lies in Alita's Shell?"

"Haven't you ever heard the expression about eggs and baskets?"

"That cannot be all."

"No, it is hardly that," she said. "I have personal reasons for seeking the queen and you will have to accept that as a minor delay in getting what you want."

"Then leave me out of this – I'll stay aboard the Hog."

"Squeamish, Thomas?"

"No."

"Come now. These men steal and kill; they bring terror to villages and towns – you saw Lanvile back there. These men are common scum, nothing more. Their lives offer nothing of value."

He had seen Lanvile where fresh graves doubled the survivors... yet Fox's threat lay heavy on his mind. "I want to do something about Fox."

She sighed. "He's probably heading out with the rest so you're wasting your time."

"No, not this man. He's a weasel; he wouldn't let himself come so close to an actual battle, even one tipped in his favour."

"If this is about Oliver, you're even more a fool. We can feed Fox something about the Orichalcum and he'll be satisfied."

"And if he isn't? If he threatens someone else – he'll keep pushing, Elisabeth."

She checked on her revolver, spinning the barrel to count the bullets, then snapping it closed. "Listen, whatever you try, you risk alerting them to that fact that we know."

"That's a risk I'm happy to take."

"By God, you are stubborn," she said with a hiss. "I'm not moving on Fox and his snakes a second before I am ready. If you want to do something useful, come with us. Or at least work the boilers or help the repair crew."

"Fine."

She pushed past him and he did not follow at once, glancing to the canyon again. *The echo of death will fill it soon enough.*

***

But despite some curiosity about the main boiler room he did not visit it, nor did he help with the repairs.

Instead, Thomas started for the map room and only when he stood within, an already open map of the Inland Federation stretched before him, lantern glowing, did he realise what he was doing.

Escape.

His situation had barely changed; if he ran, Elisabeth would likely catch him. Only now, with a reduced crew onboard, if he tried to take the steam car and water, or set out on foot, *maybe* he'd have a chance. It just meant he'd have to hide somewhere. Which in turn meant understanding the lay of the land... yet even as he lifted a lead paperweight shaped as a steam train and traced it from the canyon to a nearby forest and noted distances, roads, and town names, he knew it was a fool's errand.

How are you going to get back to the Kingdom and find Mia and Ethan? How will you free the Clara?

"This is perfect."

Thomas spun. A tall man stood in the doorway, twin-shot in hand. His expression was an unpleasant mix of glee and hatred and he was breathing hard.

As if he can't decide what to feel.

"Did you come here to use that or stare at me?" Thomas asked. The words were out almost before he could stop them.

"That all depends, freak."

"Freak?"

"That's right. I know about you. But this won't be like one bullet. Even you won't survive both barrels."

Thomas kept still, tension tightening every muscle in his body and a sharp tingling going with it. *How the hell can I keep him talking long enough to figure something out?* "Am I supposed to know who you are?"

"No. But you've taken something from me."

"What have I taken?"

"Something neither of us can have ever again now," he said, whites of his eyes showing as he lifted the barrel.

Thomas flung the paperweight.

The piece of lead flashed across the room, faster than natural. His attacker flinched away, and Thomas flew after the train, closing the distance before the man could recover. Thomas swatted the shotgun down as he dropped his shoulder, crashing into the soldier. They hit the hard floor with a grunt and rolled, grappling with one another. The man was clawing at Thomas' hands, fingernails digging into skin as they fought over the revolver belted at the man's waist.

"No!" the stranger screamed, his fury garbling the word.

Thomas found himself below the man, but he caught a wrist and squeezed until cartilage creaked. The stranger screeched, lashing out with his other hand. Blood split Thomas' lip and his head bounced off the floor. Pain spread. His vision dimmed but he heaved his entire body, flinging the man aside with a thud.

Still blinking, Thomas spun onto his knees and froze.

His enemy had landed right beside the twin-shot, even now the man was swinging it up with claw-like hands. Thomas dove away, knowing he was too slow, yet he had to try.

A deafening boom followed.

Thomas screamed at what had to be a hundred searing animal bites flashing along his side as he crashed to the floor.

And yet... he wasn't dead.

Blood flowed, staining his clothing and his ears rang, the sharp scent of gunpowder seemed everywhere, stinging his eyes, coating his tongue and burning his nostrils but he could move. *I'm alive?*

He rolled onto his back with a wince, turning his head – and flinching.

The soldier was a bloodied mess from torso to face, what little was left of it: great rents in the man's body glistened in the lamplight, deep, dark red everywhere. The pink of protruding ribs drew Thomas' eye – he couldn't look away.

Footsteps thundered along the passage above, growing nearer swiftly.

Shocked voices followed and two men in grey overalls appeared. One knelt beside Thomas, speaking, but the words were impossible to follow. The second man had lifted the blood-stained twin-shot, awe covering his face.

The barrel was bent out of shape.

When I knocked it free of the man's grip. Something must have gone wrong in the chamber.

The nearest maintenance man shook Thomas by the shoulders, voice mostly audible above the ringing. "What the bloody hell happened?"

"He tried to kill me. He... said I took something from him."

"What?"

"No idea." Thomas rubbed at his temples. "Who was he?"

"Hard to say now, I suppose."

The other fellow dropped the twin-shot onto the body. "If I had to guess I'd say it was Vincent. After all, what else could the big guy here have taken from him?"

"Ah. That might explain it."

Thomas looked between them. "I have taken nothing of his."

"Just his place," the first replied.

"His place?"

"In The Lady's bed."

Chapter 29

By evening, Elisabeth had returned with trophies for Bareo; what seemed to be a mixture of heads, weapons and loot, as best Thomas could tell from where he squinted down. She also returned with two men on stretchers and no-one called to each other in celebration or question, making it a sombre party that started up the stair leading into the Hog.

Thomas limped from Elisabeth's balcony, through the bedroom and then the dining area where he lowered himself into the chair with a grimace. He checked on his bandages, they hadn't bled through which was a relief, then fell to toying with an ivory salt shaker while he waited.

The Hog started up again before she arrived.

Her expression was flat, and blood marred one sleeve of her shirt, though she moved easily enough when she sat and appraised him. "I understand you had your own little scuffle."

"Vincent."

She leant her head back over the top of her chair. "I never thought he was that stupid. At least now we know the source of your attack."

"I suppose so," he said. And it was possible, since Fox wasn't going to try and have him killed. But there was another life at stake – Oliver. "I need to know what I'm going to tell Fox."

"Is that so urgent?" She lifted her head to look at him. "I half expected you to have questions about Vincent."

"None," Thomas said. And it was mostly true. He had no questions relating to the man as her former lover, but a thread of doubt did linger – how many other jilted lovers were aboard?

"Let me humour you then. Tell Fox that the Orichalcum is an ancient material used in alchemy, supposedly it can extend lifespan, among other things. He'll enjoy that since he or Williams would have heard that rumour."

"Is that true?"

She smiled. "It can be."

"What do you mean?"

"Precisely what I said. One use of Orichalcum was supposedly to prolong life – but I've no idea how that was supposed to be true or even if it's possible. Another use might be as a fuel source, a third is its value as a rare mineral."

"Such as?"

She shrugged. "I hardly want to estimate but the amount we carry would be worth as much as... the entire Sand-Hog herself. More maybe."

"Truly?"

"I believe so." She stood and started toward the bedroom. "Go and fetch Wilkins, will you?"

Thomas opened his mouth to reply but she was already closing the door. He nearly followed her to explain exactly what she could do with her suggestion – but instead, he rose with a grunt and left, locking the door behind him and starting toward the armoury.

The key to her rooms seemed heavy in his pocket, as though it might tear through the fabric with each step. Once again, he worked out some anger in his stride, ignoring the pain it caused his wounds. *Are you angry at yourself because you're worried about her enough to lock the door? Worried about losing the key too?*

Yet this time, he didn't let his frustration block out his surroundings, passing hissing pipes and silent cannons and their supplies, closed portholes and pale lamps with more awareness of his surroundings.

No surprises today.

But he passed the ladders to hatches, the library and dining rooms to reach the armoury without incident this time, and found Wilkins working alone, a lantern beaming from his desk. Cannon balls, rifles, shells and rounds, heavy jackets, helms and goggles loomed in shelving around them.

"Thomas? I was hoping to speak to you when I visited Lady Elisabeth actually."

"Is something wrong?"

"Perhaps." He opened a drawer and lifted a pouch free, resting it on the desk. Gleaming gold marks slid in the light. "We found this in Vincent's quarters."

Thomas whistled. "Seems a bit much, even for an officer."

"Right. My guess is that Fox – or Williams – is being quite free with his money."

"Was Vincent on your list?"

Wilkins shook his head. "No. And there was a time I would have considered bringing him into my confidence."

"Had Elisabeth done so?"

"Not to my knowledge. There are only four of us aware of Fox. Five including you."

"And you're sure Vincent attacked me on his own?"

"Lad didn't take being set aside very well at all," Wilkins said with a nod. He paused to stroke his moustache, then spread his hands. "Thomas, I understand you and The Lady have something of a fragile alliance and a... contentious past, no doubt. But to me, she is as close to a daughter as I'll ever have, and don't you let her know I said that either."

Thomas waited.

"What I'm trying to say is that I want you to protect her, if I cannot."

Thomas couldn't prevent a frown, but Wilkins kept speaking.

"No need for that. Just while your purposes align, I mean. And she can take care of herself, I think we both know that but I'm prone to worry."

What am I getting myself into? Every day it's something worse... I'm getting dragged deeper into their damn web. "So long as we share the same goals."

"Thank you." He stood. "Now, I understand you have a message to deliver and I must make my report."

"I do." *And this time, maybe I should turn some pressure back onto Fox.*

Chapter 30

Fox appeared as promised but this time, doubtless since Thomas was expecting the slimy bastard, it was without the sneak attack. The man approached, flanked by two soldiers, all wearing face wrappings, leaving only their eyes showing.

"Greetings once more, Thomas," Fox said, dark eyes narrowed – at Thomas' posture or readiness? And wasn't there something familiar about the gaze... someone from his past at the palace...

Thomas had folded his arms where he leant against one of the walls at the point where two passages met, giving him a view from two directions, two pools of light from lamps.

"Orichalcum is a rare mineral with alchemical properties – one use might be to prevent aging," he said. "Elisabeth also thinks it might be valuable as a fuel source."

His eyebrows rose, disappearing beneath the wrappings. "My, my."

Thomas pushed himself off the wall and took a single step forward. "Now I'm going to ask a question."

The muscle moved to block Thomas, but Fox waved them back. "Are you?"

"Don't worry, it's a simple one. Ready?" Thomas grinned, doing his best to make it seem as though he was privy to something Fox was not – and in a way, he was, for he'd finally put the voice and eyes together. "I need to get a message to the king. Think you can handle that?"

Fox did not speak.

"Do you need me to write it down?"

"What?"

Thomas shrugged. "Fine, just listen – I'm a little tired after catching a side full of ricocheting shot. Here it is. Ask him if he loves his bastard sons as much as his royal ones."

The man's shoulders trembled. He turned to each of his men, dismissing them. They hesitated, but he hissed an order and once they'd clomped off, Fox pointed a long finger at Thomas. "This is not a wise game, at all."

"It's the game you chose, Dane."

The man lowered his arm. "You remember me then, slave."

"Not at first." Dane had been one of many tormentors, but unlike Julian, it had been more casual than personal. Thomas had simply been one of many slaves to mistreat. Dane had been a little younger but that hadn't stopped him taking advantage of his position. "But if you don't want your secret spread between every man aboard, you'll offer me something *I* want."

"And what exactly would that be?"

"I don't trust Elisabeth. It's clear that she's using me to access Alita's Shell and after that, who knows what she'll do. Her promise to free me is as good as the sand outside. I want your word – once we break into the Shimmering Ranges and I've opened the way – you and your men will help me escape somehow."

"I see."

"I *need* to find my sister," he said. "And whatever you find in the Shell will far outweigh the cost of letting me escape."

Fox folded his arms, tapping a finger upon his bicep. "When it comes to the king, on that final point I might debate its veracity."

"I won't say you can trust me, but you have more to gain than you'd lose."

"Again, that is something I must consider," Fox said, and after a moment he turned to leave. "We will speak once more."

Thomas watched the man disappear into the shadows beyond the lamp light before slumping against the wall where he heaved a long sigh. Tension flowed from his muscles with the breath. *Did he buy it?* Deception was bloody hard on the nerves. If the snake had his doubts, things were about to get very dangerous aboard the Hog but if Fox was proud enough to want to conceal the truth about his birth, if he was greedy enough to want to claim the glory and treasures within Alita's Shell, then everything would work out.

I wish Mia were here. He frowned. *Or maybe not – I wish I could borrow her Gift and spare her from this place.*

He started back toward Elisabeth's room. She'd need to know what he'd done, for whatever misinformation she'd planned to sell, Fox would have to wait. Or be forgotten maybe, since Thomas had just set something in motion. "Dane bought it." *He has to.*

Thomas didn't need the key at Elisabeth's door, Wilkins had beaten him there and the two were already speaking over their meal – no candles this time, just lamplight. Both looked up as he entered, Wilkins appearing the same as just before, Elisabeth cleaner, her bloodied shirt replaced by a new one of similar cut.

"Something's happened," he said once he'd closed the door.

"Not another attack, I hope?" Wilkins asked.

"Worse – Fox." Thomas sat and rolled his shoulders a moment, trying to banish the remaining tension even as he winced. "His name is Dane and he's one of Williams' bastards, I finally recognised him."

Elisabeth nodded slowly. "That *is* a surprise. So, what happened? Does he doubt you?"

"No. But I had to move things along," Thomas said, then explained the lies he'd fed the man. "I think he believes me too. This is a chance to catch them in one swoop."

Her eyes flashed. "You *think* he believes you? When did I say you could think for yourself, Thomas?"

He clenched his jaw, even as his face grew hot with shame. "Let's see you open Alita's Shell by yourself then, my lady."

Wilkins cut off her reply. "Easy, you two. This can work to our favour. Nothing's changed, we've just moved the schedule up a little, the way I see it."

"Do you?" Elisabeth snapped, but she waited for him to continue.

"I do. As it stands, we dump things off for Bareo, get the queen's location and head to the ranges and spring our trap there. I remember Dane as a kid, he was a greedy little snot – he'll take the bait."

"He'd better."

"It will work. We let Thomas lead Dane and his force into a trap – I'll let one of the snakes organise a party; they'll group themselves perfectly that way."

"Who?" Elisabeth asked, even as she nodded slowly.

"Phillips."

"Good. Orders tomorrow morning; let's be ready," she said. "And tell everyone to be especially watchful now – just because we have a plan, it doesn't mean we can't be surprised."

He nodded and then excused himself.

"Tell me more about the Shimmering Ranges. What can I expect?" Thomas asked after a moment of silence.

Elisabeth tapped a finger on the table as she spoke. "From a distance they shimmer due to the granite. The lower reaches have a passage leading to the Shell, many have tried to enter but all have failed. It will take no more than an hour's trek from the point where the Hog cannot pass beyond."

"And the door?"

"It is nearly the height of the Hog itself," she said, and her tone made it clear she was not entirely present.

"Anything else?"

"Markings, most undecipherable – but I am prepared for them." She turned to face him. "Thomas, do you know specifically what the bandits did to those villages and towns?"

"No."

"Then let me spare you... but I found something within myself today that I had not realised existed. Do you know what I mean?"

He frowned. *Now she's confiding in me?* "I believe so." All he had to do was glance to the door leading to her bedchamber to remember.

"Do you know what I dreamt about as a girl?"

"No," he replied softly.

"Europa, and the New States or Asia – I wanted to travel, I was sure I'd find something better than Brinhale out there, something better than the Williams and their bitter power plays. If I could bear to look, I wouldn't find that girl within me, now."

He found himself unable to speak. *Am I actually feeling sympathy for her?* For a woman who accepted slavery, who became a part of the war machine? Who had tormented him? Mia too?

Thomas folded his arms. "I wanted to make just a single decision for myself – just one."

She faced him and there was only weariness in her tone. "Of course."

"What do you want from me, Elisabeth? Why are you telling me this?"

"Because I dare not show such weakness to anyone else."

Thomas swallowed, unable to find words – did she say such things to keep him off-balance? Because he was essentially disposable to her? Or because she actually trusted him?

She stood. "I need sleep. If you join me now, expect nothing more, Thomas."

"I will not wake you," was all he could manage.

"Thank you." Elisabeth said as she moved to her bedroom, the door clicking shut. Thomas stared after her, a deep frown settling over his face. What was she up to now? Was any of it real? He nearly kicked a chair, he nearly hurled it after her and he nearly kicked himself too, instead settling for a string of muttered curses. *What am I doing?*

Chapter 31

Mia kept busy with preparing their meal while Ethan scouted the winery.

She had arranged their foodstuffs on the bench beside the old pot-bellied stove, which had been lit earlier, and now it was just a matter of chopping up the vegetables for the stew. The sound of the knife against stone brought Delilah's home to mind and somehow, now even that time seemed a distant memory.

Because it was before Nyath and the chromata.

After the meal, she would let Ethan sleep for as long as she could stay awake and then he would once more watch over her. It *had* to work, it *had* to be enough. *I have to restore the* Clara *and rescue Thomas.* Was he even safe? There was no way to know – not with Nyath interrupting her visions. Yet she had to believe that if Thomas was in dire peril, her Gift would have found a way.

I made the right choice.

Footsteps approached in the hall and she placed a hand on the revolver Patrick had supplied, just to be safe, but

Ethan called before he opened the door. "Everything is clear outside."

"Good, let's hope it stays that way."

Over the meal, they discussed Gatehouse and possible locations on the map but made no real progress, and only loose plans to return to Viterra and start there. Supposedly, Kensington had a library to rival that of Brinhale but finding a way inside would be its own problem.

Eventually, Ethan sought his bedroll and Mia remained awake, seated at the bench, turning various useless plans over and over in her mind, the pleasant warmth of the dying fire in the stove clinging to the room but not enough to soothe her.

Nothing could, truly.

A final confrontation was looming, and she couldn't see a way to survive it – Nyath was too powerful. Nothing she had tried so far was enough, her knowledge too small, his inexplicable anger too great. *If only I had more time.*

But she didn't and the fear that only her death awaited her this night did not fade.

She clenched her hands at a wave of bitterness. *Why now? Why is this my time? What purpose does my death serve?* There was too much left unfinished; she had to find Thomas, they had to restore the *Clara* and escape together. *It felt like we were going to succeed!*

And Ethan – didn't they have a future?

"Yet you take that too," she whispered, though she did not know to whom or what exactly. Supposed Gods that presided over a broken land? Nyath? The failures of her Farsight?

But there was a thing that could not be taken.

Mia drew in a shuddering breath and slipped from the makeshift chair, moving softly to Ethan's side. Once there, she stopped. *Why are you hesitating? You know how he feels.* Still she didn't reach out, because it was clear. *This is about how I feel.* Despite her resolve, uncertainty froze her limbs. Taking that first step would lead to the next, and then to somewhere she had never gone. *Will it hurt? Will it be wonderful, like in stories? Will I even know what to do? Will he be gentle?*

She had to trust him.

Stop hesitating, fool – this is your last night, isn't it?

Sudden tears built, and she wiped them away then bent closer to place her hand on Ethan's cheek, the stubble coarse beneath her palm.

He stirred immediately. "Mia?"

"Nothing is wrong," she said, then leant closer still, letting her lips brush against his. They were soft and warm, and she closed her eyes to stop more tears as his arms slipped up around her, pulling her atop his chest. His body was firm, his grip strong, and together their kiss deepened.

Ethan's arms tightened, his kiss becoming a little heated and she pulled back, almost an instinct. Yet it wasn't blind fear; she didn't want to be afraid, half of it was shock at her own response to his need. "Not too fast," she said.

He was breathing harder than she. "You're right."

Ethan reached up to cup her face and then slid the blindfold free, letting his finger tips trail across her cheeks and even eyelids, the sensation sending shivers along her entire body.

But he stopped.

"You've been crying."

"No, this is what I want." She kissed him again and as she did, she ran her hands across his bare torso, he'd already removed it to sleep, the muscles rippling beneath her touch. Ethan's own hands slipped beneath her shirt, running across her back as he pulled her close once more.

***

Mia woke to the chromata, now a world of night with another bone-white moon leeching the colour from her surroundings; she stood in a ballroom with a mighty chandelier overhead, shaped as a teardrop. The room was lined with floor-to-ceiling windows, each one filled by criss-crossing grilles and between each window in turn, enormous lilies in tall vases.

Diamond patterns from the moonlight hit the polished marble floor as she started forward, footfalls echoing. *When did I fall asleep? Is Ethan watching over me?* Her pulse was already quickening, the sense of lying with him fading, the rush of emotions drifting away too – as if it never happened, leaving her alone once more.

Yet her fear was not so strong as before.

Because I've accepted my fate?

Or because I won't go without a fight?

She spun where she stood but the ballroom was empty. "Nyath? Come and find me, you bastard."

"I am here, interloper."

His red robe had faded to grey where he stood at the opposite end of the ballroom floor, the eyes in his skull already bleeding their shadows.

"This, tonight is the end for one of us," she said.

"That I know." He started to glide forward, legs still missing. *Is he toying with me now? He hasn't bothered lately.*

"Then if it is so, answer me a question," she demanded. "Who are you truly?"

He did not slow. "Upon my death and no sooner."

If I must fall, I refuse to cower before the end.

Mia charged.

As she ran, she drove her determination and hatred of him into her fists, the fury setting her arms and hands to pulsing. Nyath raised his own limbs as he neared. Mia swung a blow just as Nyath attacked, and the pent-up force between them crashed together with a thunderclap.

Mia was thrown back.

She hit the marble with a grunt, sliding across the floor, but she leapt to her feet as soon as she could. Nyath was already standing – he flickered out of sight. Mia swung both fists on instinct, striking the man as he appeared directly before her.

He roared as the blow drove him back, but just as quickly, he snapped from view. Mia whirled, arms raised to strike but he was too fast this time, catching her in a vice-like grip. His arms began to crush her torso and her ribs creaked, forcing a scream into the night.

Mia rained blows upon the skull but could not break the mask.

"You are out of friends at last," he growled.

Mia kept striking him but her blows were slowing – the robed killer was right, she was alone. No-one could help her now; not Thomas as always, not Ethan who'd done so since, not Patrick and not the Guide either.

Yet wasn't there another?

Mia drove her elbows downwards now, striking Nyath's grip once, twice, and finally, on the third blow, winning her freedom. She hit the marble and flung her arms at her enemy. "Back!"

All her anger and desperation surged out with the word. Nyath flew across the room as if taken by the wind, yet he did not crash through the wall or window, instead, he regained his balance and descended lightly to the ground.

"Not strong enough, girl."

But Mia was already singing the old lullaby, calling on the Bird of Light with the wordless melody, raising her voice to echo across the ballroom.

A shrill cry split the air.

Glass shattered outwards as the blinding, fiery light appeared, driving Nyath back. Mia opened her mouth to command the searing bird but it disappeared and Mia's body began to hum. She raised her hands only to find they glowed, golden rays shooting forth.

How? But it didn't matter.

Mia looked across the room.

Nyath rose from his crouch and for the first time, she saw fear in his bearing – his shoulders trembled. "This cannot be."

"You are wrong about that." Mia raised her hand. A bolt of light streaked forth with a crack that rocked the ballroom. It struck his chest, exploding in a shower of golden sparks and she hurled another and then another until she had to stop, suddenly out of breath.

Yet when the light was gone there was no Nyath, only a shrivelled black cloud remained and the echo of a rasping howl, fading into silence.

The horned skull clattered to the marble.

Mia crossed the floor, a fist of light still held ready as she neared but there were no surprises. The robe was gone, the shadows too. All that remained was a cracked skull, fragments of bone nearby – and no answer as to his identity.

Is that the end of him then?

There was no way to know whether she'd banished him or only won a temporary battle, but her instincts – or her Farsight – told her she had struck him a heavy blow nonetheless and that for now at the very least, the chromata was safe once more.

She glanced at to the ceiling, where the chandelier caught the light that poured from her body – not just her hands but even her eyes and mouth as she spoke, new belief coursing through her.

"Thank you for your blessing, Great One."

Chapter 32

For their second visit to the highway governor, Thomas found himself squinting in the sun-lit office, sitting beside Elisabeth who was now her usual self – but how much of that was a front? *Damn her, she's put too much doubt into my head now.* Whatever acts she'd committed in the canyon had obviously taken their toll, but it was impossible to see that now, as she fixed Bareo with a stern look.

"I cannot read this, Governor." She gestured to the sheet of paper he'd placed before her.

"Forgive my eccentricity – or paranoia, whichever you prefer – but the code is quite simple. The first two letters refer to a Federation city, the next two refer to a month, and the final pair obviously corresponds with the individual's name."

Thomas glanced at the paper – the two letters for city were v and a... which made it Vanwood if he remembered Elisabeth's map correctly, a major city but not the capital. Located somewhere south west of the ranges.

Elisabeth folded the paper and tucked it into her shirt as

she stood. "And what of Felicity?"

He chuckled. "I'm afraid you'll have to ask your men about that; I made a promise."

"Such nobility," she said, seemingly unperturbed by his knowledge of her activities.

"Guilty, I must admit. And will our usual arrangement be in effect during your next visit?"

"Doubtless I will have no more luck than I have in the past," she said with a nod.

"Until then," Bareo said. He glanced at Thomas, then back to Elisabeth. "Unless you'd care to join me for a meal when you pass through?"

"I'll need more than a decent meal for your offer to be tempting," she said, motioning for Thomas to follow as she started for the door.

"Like an arrow in my heart," he grinned.

In the stone hallway, Elisabeth quickened her pace. His wounds were healing well enough that he could keep up but it wasn't without some effort. "I want to hear what Oliver has to say about the queen's maid."

"Why do you think the queen wants to contact someone from the Kingdom?"

"I have no idea, but I'd very much like to know. Whatever the reason, it will have to wait until I'm finished with the Shell. Vanwood is two weeks away."

"But that doesn't mean the queen is."

"Let's see what young Felicity revealed, first," she said as she exited the building.

A pair of servants – not slaves – were tending to Bareo's garden, white-flowering vines covering the walls of the courtyard. He could have paused; the scent of the unfamiliar flower was present too. Mia would have loved it.

They joined the colourful flow of Federation and former Kingdom citizens in the streets, the pleasant sound of Federation accents washing over him as he looked to the town walls. The Sand-Hog was just visible beyond, faint plumes of steam crawling up the sky. Wilkins would have everything ready to head north, supplies and extra water taken on while Elisabeth delivered her evidence to Bareo.

At the gates, two soldiers in black flak jackets waited – Oliver and the other man she'd sent to tail Felicity.

"My lady," Oliver said. "We've finished with our tasks and thought we'd report now, if we saw you."

"A little closer to the Hog then," she said.

Once they'd left the streets and started across the plain toward the not-too-distant Sand-Hog, Oliver outlined their efforts.

"We didn't learn much, I'm afraid. She met a well-armed man within the gates and they entered a nice place on the other side of town. We've marked the building but she never left the whole time."

"Only saw her at the window once," the second man said.

"But Felicity is still here?"

Oliver nodded. "As of earlier today, at least. We wanted to tell you in case you wanted to pick her up?"

She slowed. "No, not this time. I'm curious but not that curious – we're too close to Alita's Shell. If she's here when we return, we'll figure it out then. Good work."

Oliver beamed, and the other man seemed equally pleased.

When they reached the Hog, Elisabeth sent them off to report to Sergeant Wilkins and nearly dragged Thomas along the passages to the mess hall where she ordered food then sat across from him at a table set off from the others, though the hall was otherwise empty.

"Why are you rushing?" he asked.

"We have a lot to organise," she said. "Get something to eat here and then I want you to make yourself accessible to Fox, doesn't matter how. He'll no doubt be watching for our return anyway. Then join Wilkins and I in my rooms. We'll wait."

"What if—"

"Just make it happen, Thomas," she said as she left.

And then he was alone.

Thomas nearly followed, perhaps a walk along the corridors where Fox usually lurked but waiting right where he was would probably be just as effective. No major meal loomed just yet and so anything he had to say to Fox would go unheard beneath whatever preparation the cooks were undertaking.

"Here is your meal," a soft voice said.

Fox stood before him, face still concealed by a scarf, holding a tray of bread and cheese and apple. *How does the bastard move so quietly?*

Thomas accepted the tray. "Join me, Dane."

The man did not sit. "What do you want?"

"You take care of Elisabeth. Afterwards, give me supplies and the steam car; I'll be heading further inland at first, so I want access to a road. Most of them in the Federation seem quite well-maintained, any will do."

"Not chasing your sister, then?"

"Who said I'm not?" Thomas replied, biting into one of the apple wedges. Not bad. "So, do we have a deal?"

"You'll lead Elisabeth into our trap."

"No, I'll *send* her wherever you say but I'm not getting involved in the crossfire. Too easy for accidents to happen that way."

"Do you really think she'll buy it if you don't go with her?" Thomas shook his head.

"Then consider our deal finished," Fox said, turning to leave.

"Wait."

He turned back. "Yes?"

"Fine. Just make sure your men shoot straight."

"You won't be our target, believe me," he said, some venom creeping into his voice. "Lead her into the canyon before the entry; we'll take up positions in the rocks. Get to the great doors as soon as possible and you'll miss most of the bullets."

"And then I have my car and the supplies, and you take me to the nearest road," Thomas said.

"Yes."

Thomas pointed his fork at the man. "Yes. Remember, *Dane* – I know your secret."

"Just live up to your side of the bargain, slave," Fox snapped as he headed for the kitchen. Thomas glared at the man as he left, taking another bite. *The little bastard is going to try and double-cross me.*

Chapter 33

The Shimmering Ranges twisted up out of rocky hills, their peaks and sides dark, streaked with pale yellow and grey too. At present, despite the harsh sun, they did not shimmer at all. And while they hardly challenged the clouds, they were no mere hillside either.

Thomas hitched his pack and glanced back along the weaving trail and its line of soldiers to the Sand-Hog. It stood like a black beast at the edge of usable earth, the tread had managed some pretty rough terrain at first but when it finally reached its limit Elisabeth gave the order to set out on foot, leaving a skeleton crew behind.

Now, Thomas trudged behind Elisabeth, Oliver and Wilkins, Phillips and another man with them, tension slowly building as they neared what Elisabeth had explained was the final stretch, where she called a halt. They now stood on an even plateau that was partially enclosed by rock walls, there were faint traces of previous camps too; a large fire pit and faint gouges for tent pegs nearby.

"All right, sergeants, I want this staging-area established

and then a scouting party for the Shell organised; we don't want any surprises."

"I'll start on the camp," Wilkins said. "I want to check on the drill before we go any further."

Phillips nodded as he signalled to the line of soldiers that were filing in, raising his voice. "Volunteers for scouting – no complaints, either."

Despite the discomfort it caused, Thomas helped Wilkins arrange their supplies, some of which were parts for a huge drill and its boiler, keeping an eye on the scouting party as he did. They were, he had to assume, all or mostly men Phillips wanted. None appeared to be Dane, but then, it was hard to tell with the helmets and goggles, not that the wind was whipping up too much dust.

Once the last man had left, heading for the trail that curved up and around, Elisabeth approached and lowered her voice. "Ready to take the final step?"

Wilkins nodded. "If Fox wants a clean coup, he'll have taken them all for the trap – we outnumber him, he'll need all the firepower he can get."

"Yes, but that doesn't mean he won't leave a few behind here, to be sure."

"I have our best men watching," he said.

"Very well. Give the order."

Thomas couldn't help holding his breath as a second wave of men followed – only they started out on a different path, meaning to take up positions above Dane's men. Whether it would work... Thomas had no way of judging, he hadn't seen the terrain around the entry, but Elisabeth was confident in that part at least.

Yet any one of these men left behind could be one of the snakes.

"He expects me to lead you into his trap," Thomas said. "We haven't talked about this part."

"Just finish up here and then we walk right in, Wilkins' men will have it under control if we give them enough time to get into position."

"That's all? No hidden ace up your sleeve?"

She shook her head. "We gamble it all on this ploy."

Thomas continued his work on one of many tents until Wilkins called for a halt, gathering everyone into a line. "Lead on, Thomas," he said, and Elisabeth joined him at the start. They all bore rifles, additional ammunition belts with their water flasks, and more. Several men carried tools like pick axes, shovels along with gunpowder and ropes. *Just what does she think we'll find inside?*

They did not speak during the half-hour climb, not until near the end, when Elisabeth ordered all non-essential items be offloaded temporarily then slapped Thomas on the back. "Ready?"

"I suppose I have to be."

"Don't worry, The Lady will triumph," Oliver said.

Wilkins gave his own nod of agreement. "Our lads will aim true, don't you worry about that."

I just have to worry about whether they shoot every one of the snakes. He could probably take a bullet or two and survive; after all, he had in the past, but that didn't mean he'd be able to survive three... or ten... or twenty. Or even *one* in the heart. Or head.

"Just around this corner," Elisabeth said.

The rock walls had climbed up around them now, funnelling everyone toward a wide opening. This close, the granite walls did glimmer beneath the sun, but it was the open space beyond that drew Thomas' eye.

Broad enough for at least a hundred men, it was dominated by the giant gateway set into the very mountain, a towering steel pair of double doors at least four-storeys tall. It seemed covered in markings or runes, but Thomas didn't approach. They stopped a little ways before it, Elisabeth at his side, Wilkins opposite and the rest of the men filing in behind.

"Throw down your weapons," a gruff voice shouted, echoing around the enclosed plateau.

Phillips.

Dozens of men in black rose from positions above, rifles pointed downward where they encircled Elisabeth's force, faces grim. One figure did not aim his weapon yet – Dane. The man still wore his face coverings but there was triumph in his voice.

"You have one chance to surrender now, we have the advantage," he called. "If you want to survive, give up the Lady Elisabeth and you can rejoin the Hog and join us. Otherwise, we slaughter you all."

Thomas frowned. He'd half expected an instant gunfight, but it seemed Dane wanted something.

Elisabeth raised her own voice. "Dane, you little worm. Couldn't face me openly?"

"You're finished, bitch. Now, where is the control key? Tell us and we make it quick, otherwise I search every inch of your body with my knife."

"I see." She shrugged, then gave a shout. "Positions!"

More men, hidden yet higher, some on quite precarious footing, rose to train their own weapons on Dane's traitors. Yet Fox did not even glance up, nor did most of his fellow snakes – instead, he only grinned.

Something's wrong.

"Oh my, you have us now, don't you?" Dane almost purred the words.

A new voice spoke. "Sorry, my lady, but you have betrayed my king."

Thomas spun.

Oliver stood behind Elisabeth, a revolver pressed against her back. Rather than shock, it was sadness that covered her face. "You too, Oliver?"

"You have to decide how you want this to end," he said, his young face tight with repressed emotion. Was it loathing or disappointment? *Does it matter? Think of something, fool.*

"Well, what will it be?" Dane shouted down.

"I want your oath," Elisabeth replied. "That my men will not be killed."

Thomas closed his eyes as Dane and Elisabeth continued to negotiate – he couldn't shoot everyone, he could flee and despite the reluctance to admit it, he didn't want them to slaughter Elisabeth. *What can I do? For all my strength, the questionable gifts from Silas, I'm just one man against many.*

But wasn't that the answer? He was one man, but he was the only one of his kind.

I can feel their weapons.

All around Thomas, the sense of steel was strong; not just the enormous doors but every rifle, revolver, helmet and set of goggles, and even their belt buckles... he relaxed the restraints he'd long-since put up, for every moment aboard the Hog, it seemed, and simply let his body react to all the weapons.

The tingling became a humming, a song of steel coupled

with buzzing in his ears, one that increased swiftly. He grimaced; the worst of it came from the gate but there was a sense of being... rebuffed, as though his senses couldn't actually penetrate.

But the weapons were far more receptive. *I need to get rid of them...*

Thomas opened his eyes, and swallowed as he further lowered his restrains, moving from being *open* to the metal, to seeking it, to *calling* it to him – as if his body were giving off a deep, resonant chime that attracted the steel.

A shudder ran through him as he urged it all down toward him.

Cries echoed around the clearing.

Men were cursing, their faces full of shock and pain as rifles, revolvers, helms and small pieces of steel leapt free. Many men gripped bleeding hands as they fell back, had they lost trigger fingers?

The steel was streaking across the air toward Thomas. He raised his hands and the pieces stopped, clacking and crashing together. Sparks flashed as more and more pieces shot across the space and collided, until a mass of bristling steel finally hung before him and a hush fell across those gathered, broken only by occasional whimpering.

He couldn't prevent himself from gaping.

How long would it hang there?

Thomas kept himself open to the steel as he looked around. Elisabeth stood over Oliver, who lay sprawled on the ground, wiping at a bloody lip. Wilkins was marshalling his men and new shouts of pain and thuds echoed from the walls as Dane's men were overwhelmed, some thrown down to land with sharp cracks from broken bones.

"Well done, Thomas," Elisabeth said, resting a hand on his shoulder. "I knew you'd come up with something."

He glared at her. "What?"

"You were always my ace, but I wasn't going to say anything, just in case Dane had left a snake behind – which he did."

Thomas shook his head. "*I* didn't even know this was possible. How did you?"

"I didn't know this specifically. But I knew you'd be the difference."

"You took a huge risk."

"Really? I hadn't realised."

"I meant with *my* life," he snapped.

"Don't forget that you escalated this, Thomas. I hadn't planned to move on Fox until Wilkins was done with his work."

He met her unwavering gaze. Pointless to argue.

"Fine. Just tell me when I can put this down, then."

Chapter 34

This time Mia woke with a pleasant heaviness to her limbs, as though she'd had her first true rest in weeks. She did not immediately stir; she simply lay still, listening to the rustle of pages from Ethan, obviously studying the plan still, until her stomach caused her to rise, searching for her clothes and then blindfold with her hands, despite the dark kitchen posing little threat to her sensitive eyes.

"Good morning," Ethan said. "I think you actually slept this time, am I right?"

"Yes." She stood and moved toward him, her hand outstretched – not for balance but to touch him again. His hand met hers and she smiled. "Nyath is defeated."

He squeezed her hand. "I knew you could do it, Mia."

"At least one of us was sure," she said, explaining about the Bird of Light and Nyath's refusal to reveal his true nature. "And I wouldn't have succeeded without you."

"And last night... before?" he asked.

She reached up to touch his cheek, then pulled him into a kiss. "Was wonderful; you needn't fear."

"Good." She caught a trace of relief in his words. "Then let's not rush breakfast. And we have to plan our next move, right?"

"We should start with Viterra." Mia found one of the seats they'd fashioned from the wreckage in the winery.

"There's water there," Ethan said as he rummaged about in his pack.

Mia moved a hand across the bench and stopped when she encountered the flask, drinking deeply. "The quicker we can confirm or rule it out the better."

"I've been thinking about that too," he said as the strong scent of ashes being stirred reached her. "I can probably weasel my way in to Lord Kensington's good graces, but it will take time. It might be easier if I sneak in."

"How? And do you know where the maps are held?"

"I guess we'd figure that one when we return. I still have a few people who owe me favours in the city." He paused. "The bigger question is probably what we do once we have the starting point or translations for other names – do we follow the map or seek out Thomas?"

Mia lowered her flask. There was no easy answer to that question, but her Farsight would provide more clues, surely, now that Nyath was gone. "I want to find him, but I don't know what's changed. At least my visions should return – we should be able to decide from there."

"And if the worst has come to pass?" Ethan asked softly.

"It hasn't," Mia said – but she didn't know and that was her hope speaking. *You'd better not be in any more trouble, brother.*

"Then we'll return to Brightnest and plan our journey from there. Perhaps by then, you'll know a little more."

Mia nodded. She still needed to decide on a new leader too but for now, it was hard not to worry more about Thomas. "By tonight, I'm sure I'll learn something new, Ethan."

Chapter 35

Once Dane and his men were bound and set under guard – those that survived the counter-coup – Elisabeth called for Thomas but he did not go to her at once, instead, he paused before The Fox where the royal bastard sat slumped against the rock face in the dying light of evening, surrounded by his conspirators.

"Come to gloat then?" Dane asked, bitterness clear in his voice.

"Yes." But Thomas didn't smile. Instead, he knelt and met the man's gaze. "In case you don't survive whatever Elisabeth has in mind, I thought we'd better take this chance to talk – after all, you seem to love our little talks."

Dane narrowed his eyes. "What do you want?"

"Exactly this," Thomas said. "To see what you've made of yourself here today."

The Fox lunged forward, arms bound behind his back, but Thomas simply shoved the man down with a sneer, then rose to walk away, ignoring the man's incoherent cursing.

"Finished playing?" Elisabeth asked when he joined her

before the giant door.

"I think so." He looked up. As he'd estimated, the door was at least four-storeys tall. It was covered in markings, most of which were illegible to him but the Gatehouse symbol was prominent enough, though when he stretched up to run a hand across the bottom of the hourglass, he frowned.

"This was added later," he said.

"So I suspect."

He pointed to the smooth, twisting runes higher up. "And things like those ones... I could almost feel their age through the door, they predate Gatehouse."

Elisabeth smiled. "Indeed."

"What?"

"While I didn't need more proof exactly, it's certainly a comfort to have my suspicion confirmed – I knew hunting you all those years was the right choice."

"You must be thrilled," he said through clenched teeth.

"Indeed. Now what of these?" she asked, gesturing to a row of triangular-shaped alcoves set into the door. They were half as big as his head and spanned the entirety of both wings, numbering twenty at least.

"No idea."

"That's not what I'm paying you for."

"Paying me?"

"Yes. Your life, your eventual freedom – that's your payment."

He knelt and reached within an alcove, feeling around. There was a small opening at the back, as if for a key, but the floor of each space bore twin grooves. Not too deep, but very regular in shape. "Do they all bear the same grooves?" he asked as he ran a hand across one. Like three lines, splayed.

"All are identical."

"Hmmm." He rose. "I don't know what they're for, but I can try and open the gate if you like. I don't know if cutting through will damage it in some way?"

"Nor I, but I'm willing to risk that."

He started rubbing his hands together to build the friction and heat. "Have you ever tried to blast through the stone?"

"Yes, but it was useless, the mountain is too strong – it's unnatural. What little we managed only revealed more door or walls, as if the stone has somehow grown up around this place. I can't even guess at how thick it is. You remember what the door at the *Clara* was like."

"I do." He kept working until the tingling and heat were painful, then reached forth… and nothing. The steel did not respond. He beat against it once, twice, and thrice but it made no difference. No markings appeared and even when he tried to grip and tear at the small alcoves, he couldn't so much as bend it even a tiny bit out of shape.

He slammed his fist against it a few more times for good measure before stepping back to catch his breath. "It's impossible."

Elisabeth was pacing, her jaw clenched. "Is that all you can do?"

"Take your turn, my lady."

She stopped to fold her arms. "You were supposed to be the last piece of the blasted puzzle! I chased you all the way to that train wreck and then the village of runaways and finally Viterra, I chased you across the entire bloody Kingdom and nothing!"

"Wait…" Thomas raised a hand. Something tugged at his

memory... the wreck of *Esmeralda*? And Mia. Mia singing. And dozens of mechanical birds singing too! *Could it be? Did David know all along – is that why he sent us to the train?*

"What?"

"I have an idea but I don't know... I think David was trying to tell us something."

"Tell you what?"

"That the *Esmeralda* was more important than we thought. We might have another long journey before us."

"Why?" Her fury had eased, replaced by eagerness as she leant closer.

"There were a host of mechanical birds hidden in one of the carriages. I think they fit here," he said, waving an arm at the alcoves. *And that's what those grooves are for, bird claws.* "I think we need them."

She grinned. "I have them already."

"You what?"

"We looted the train. The birds are sitting in the hold of the Hog."

He blinked.

"Let's get them here," she said, and turned to her men, hollering her orders.

When they finally returned, carrying two long wooden boxes, the light was low enough that torches and lanterns had to be lit. Enough burnt now to set the gateway to gleaming, the hourglass prominent. *Is this how you found a way inside, Gatehouse?*

"Start at that end," Elisabeth said, lifting one of the intricately constructed mechanical birds free of the first box. Thomas nodded and dragged his box across the earth, then started on his own birds. Heavy and cold, each one was a marvel but he placed them within each alcove without delay, holding his breath at first. The clawed feet fit the grooves snugly, locking the bird in place. He soon met Elisabeth where both doors joined.

Together, they stood back and waited, murmuring from the watching soldiers growing softer.

Nothing.

Thomas stepped forward and pushed on the doors, but they did not budge.

"Any other ideas, Thomas?" Elisabeth asked, her tone starting to darken again.

"In the *Esmeralda*, Mia made them sing but..." he trailed off. *Idiot!*

Elisabeth caught his arm. "Your sister made them sing, you say?"

Fool! Fool! Fool!

"Thomas."

No lie will work now – you're a stupid, stupid man, Thomas. He'd let his desire for freedom cloud his mind and worse, his loyalty. "Yes. There's a lullaby she knows but she could be anywhere by now – it'll be almost impossible to find her."

"Now, now, Thomas," she said with a grin. "It wouldn't do to give up before we've even started."

A Note from Ashley

Hi! I hope you enjoyed *The Ruby Heart* and thanks for joining Thomas and Mia once more.

I'd like to ask if you could help me out by leaving an honest review of the story at your place of purchase? Long or short, bad or good, it all helps!

AND if you'd like to sign up to my newsletter (www. ashleycapes.com) you'll be the first to know when the third *Slaves of the New World* book is released. You'll also have first access to preview chapters and pre-release editions of the story, in addition to being automatically added into the draw for giveaways.

Ashley

ACKNOWLEDGMENTS

Thanks again to the huge cast of folks who helped me with my latest release.

I must of course thank my wife Brooke for her endless support but also my writing group, the Alchemists, along with my editor Amanda and also Nick Deligaris for yet another stunning cover image! Thanks also to Vivid for the superb typeset too and also to those of you who spent your time with my characters!

Ashley

ABOUT ASHLEY

Ashley Capes is an Australian novelist, poet and teacher. He teaches English, Media and Music Production, has played in a metal band, worked in an art gallery and slaved away at music retail. Aside from reading and writing, Ashley loves volleyball and Studio Ghibli – and *Magnum PI*, easily one of the greatest television shows ever made.

Visit his blogs www.ashleycapes.com or follow him on twitter @Ash_Capes.

Fiction

The Bone Mask Trilogy
1. *City of Masks*
2. *The Lost Mask*
3. *Greatmask*

Book of Never
1. *The Amber Isle*
2. *A Forest of Eyes*
3. *River God*
4. *The Peaks of Autumn*
5. *Imperial Towers*
6. *The Phoenix of Kiymako*

www.ingramcontent.com/pod-product-compliance
Lightning Source LLC
Chambersburg PA
CBHW030642110726
47901CB00002B/542